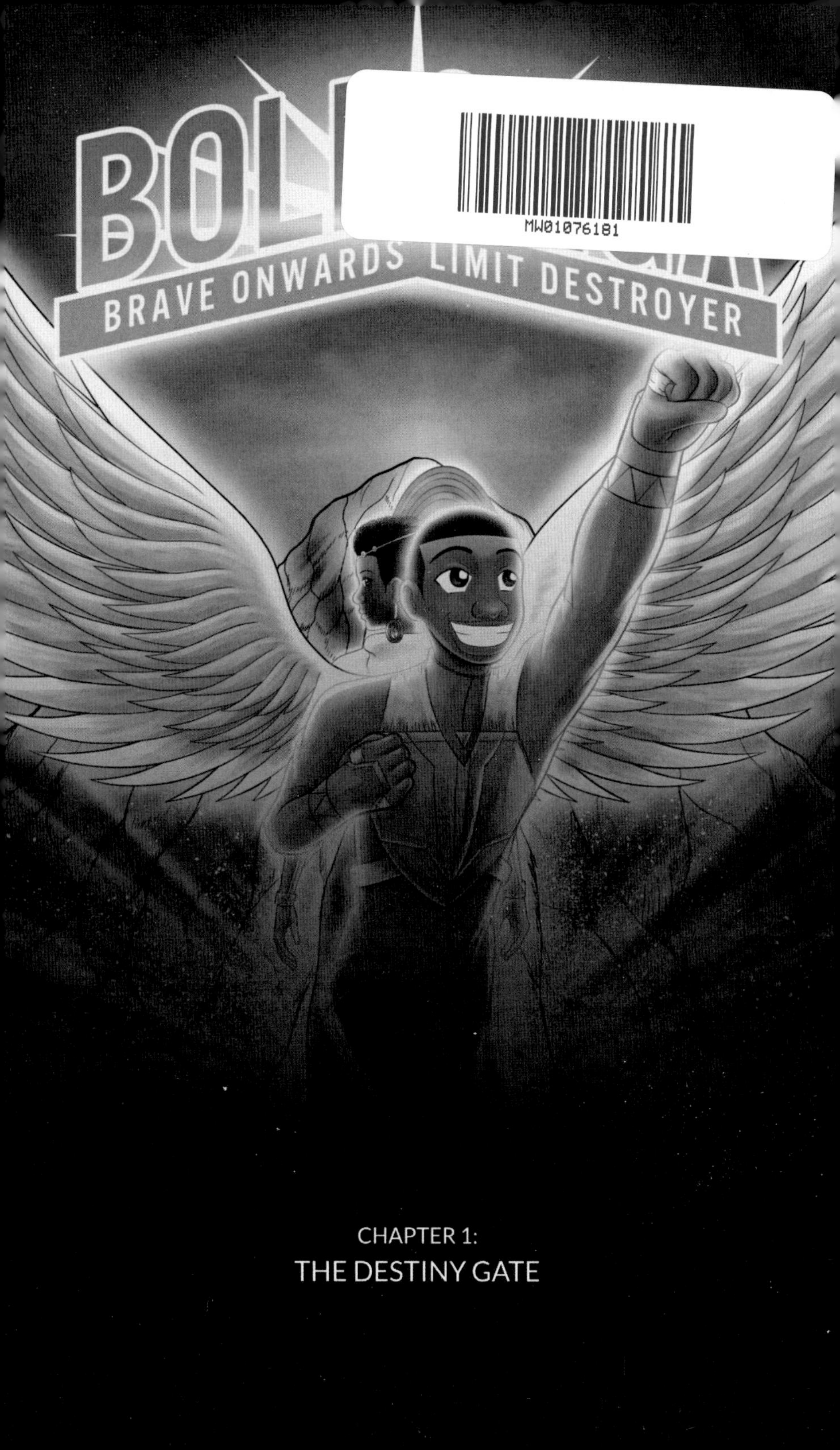
BRAVE ONWARDS LIMIT DESTROYER

CHAPTER 1:

THE DESTINY GATE

BOLDSAGA
BRAVE ONWARDS LIMIT DESTROYER
CHAPTER 1:
THE DESTINY GATE

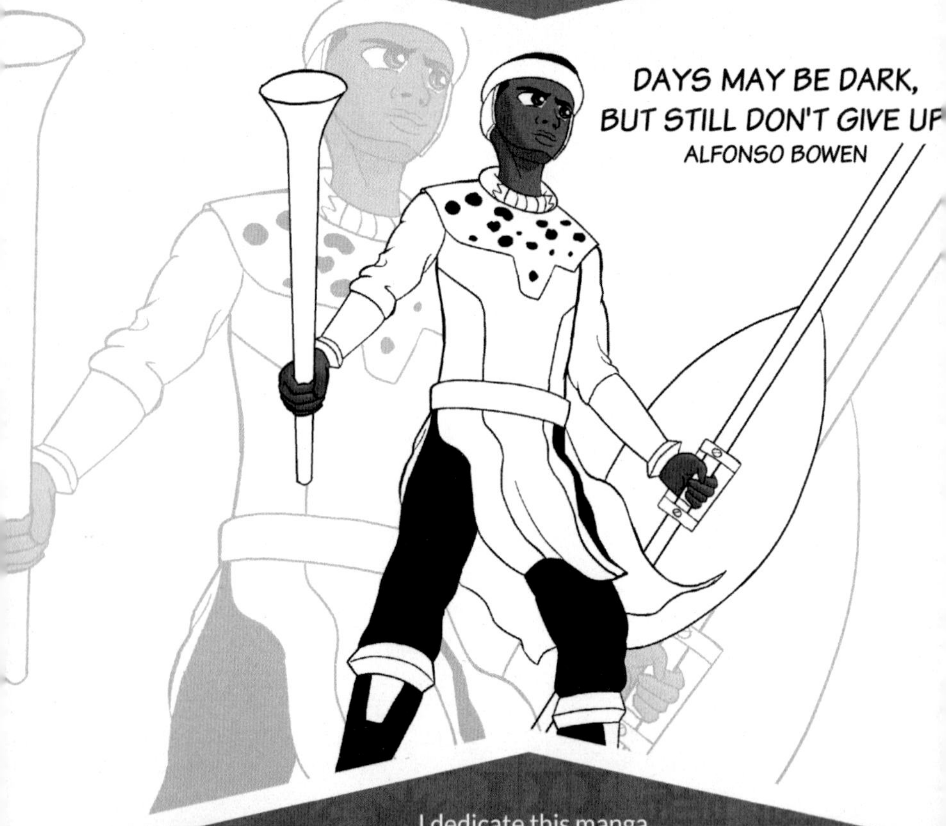
DAYS MAY BE DARK, BUT STILL DON'T GIVE UP
ALFONSO BOWEN

I dedicate this manga
to God, my wife Tamara, Rochelle,
Ewart, Rosalie, Brandon, De'shaun, Derek, Jean, my family, friends

First published in New York by Great Gale LLC.

Published by Great Gale, LLC
P.O. Box 344
Poughkeepsie, New York, 12602

www.greatgale.com

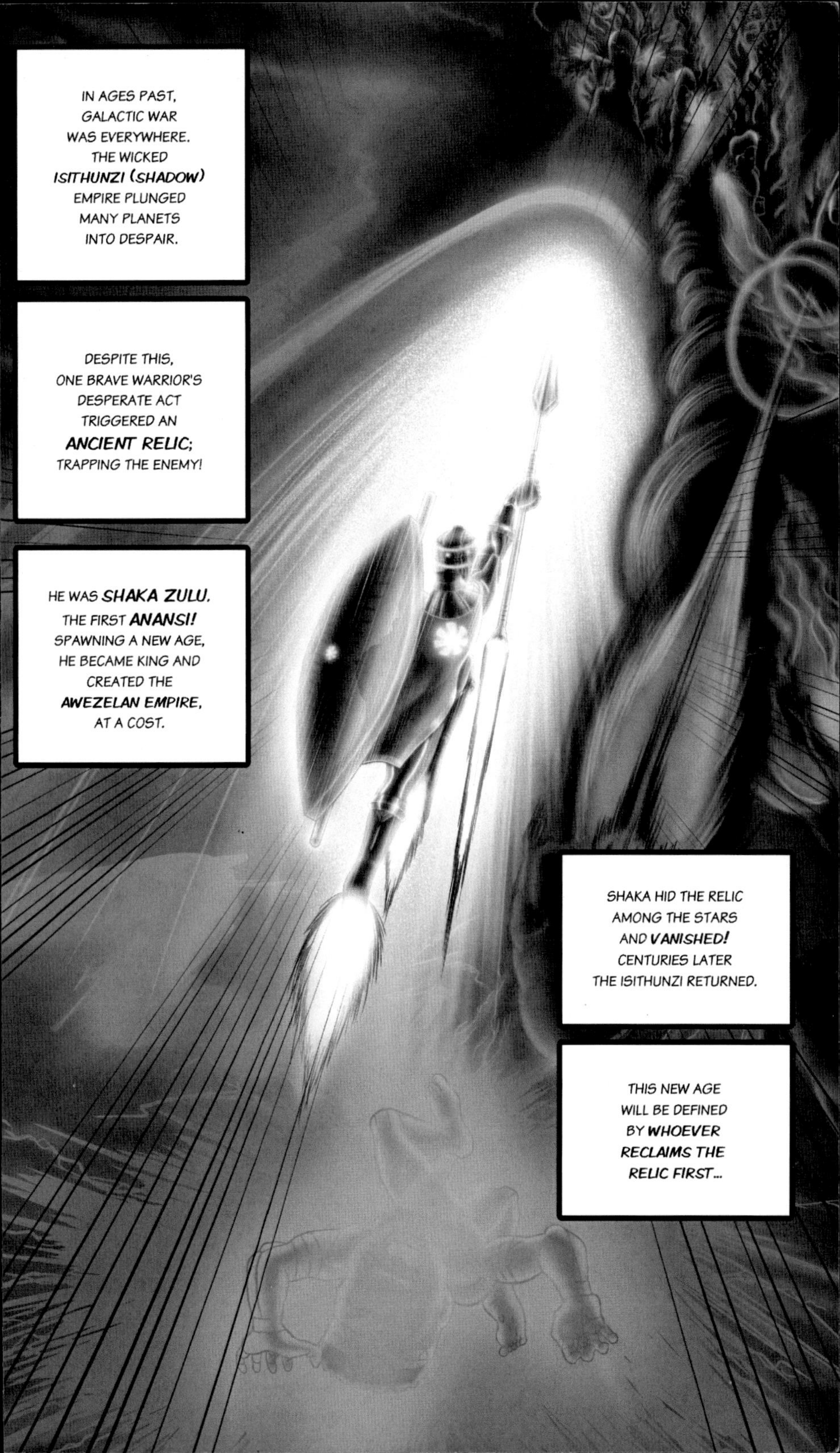
IN AGES PAST, GALACTIC WAR WAS EVERYWHERE. THE WICKED ISITHUNZI (SHADOW) EMPIRE PLUNGED MANY PLANETS INTO DESPAIR.
DESPITE THIS, ONE BRAVE WARRIOR'S DESPERATE ACT TRIGGERED AN ANCIENT RELIC; TRAPPING THE ENEMY!
HE WAS SHAKA ZULU, THE FIRST ANANSI! SPAWNING A NEW AGE, HE BECAME KING AND CREATED THE AWEZELAN EMPIRE, AT A COST.
SHAKA HID THE RELIC AMONG THE STARS AND VANISHED! CENTURIES LATER THE ISITHUNZI RETURNED.
THIS NEW AGE WILL BE DEFINED BY WHOEVER RECLAIMS THE RELIC FIRST...

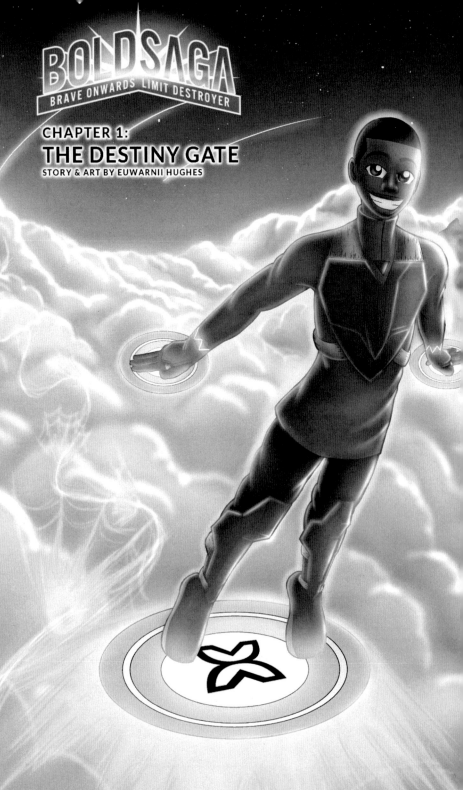

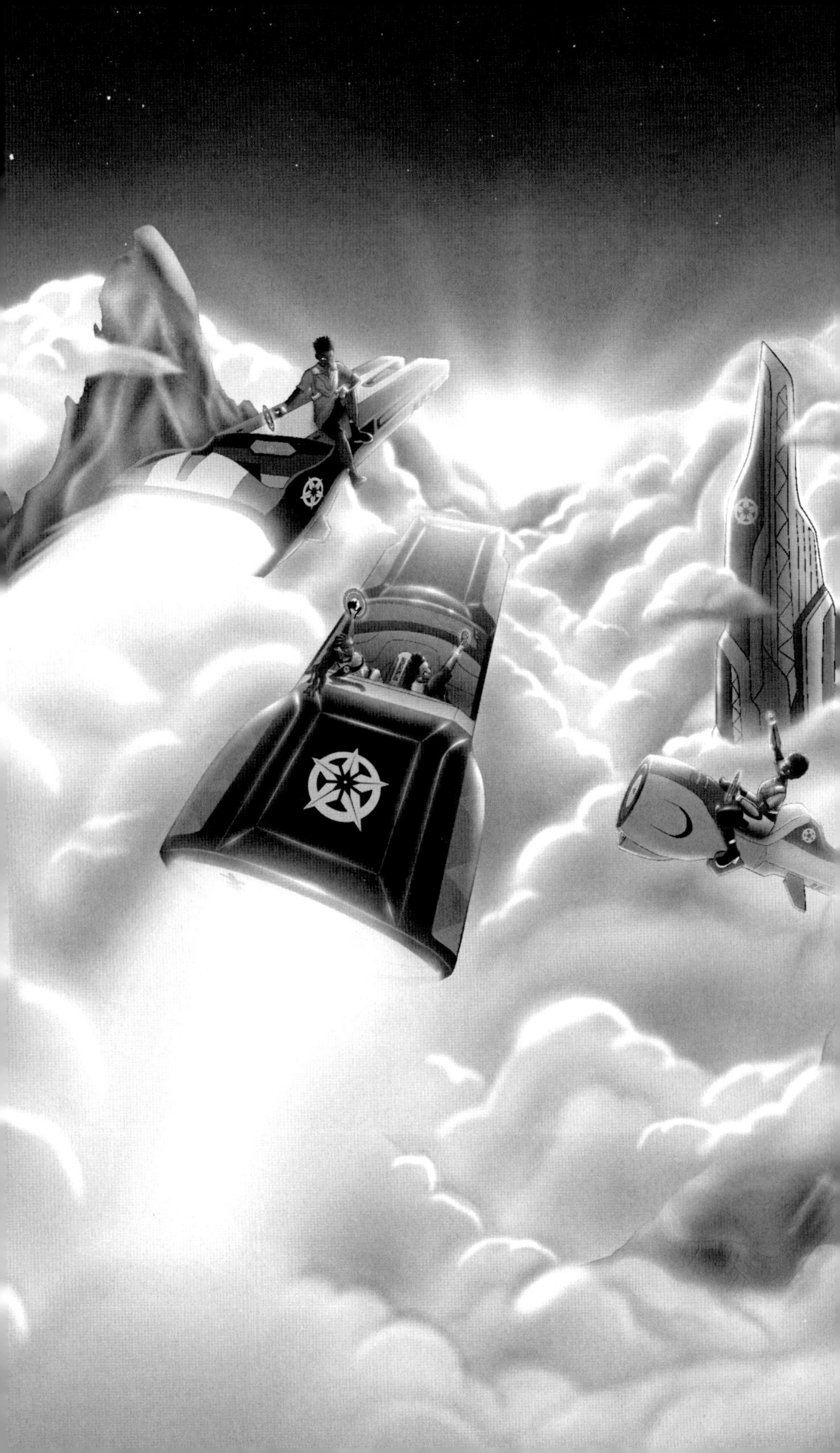

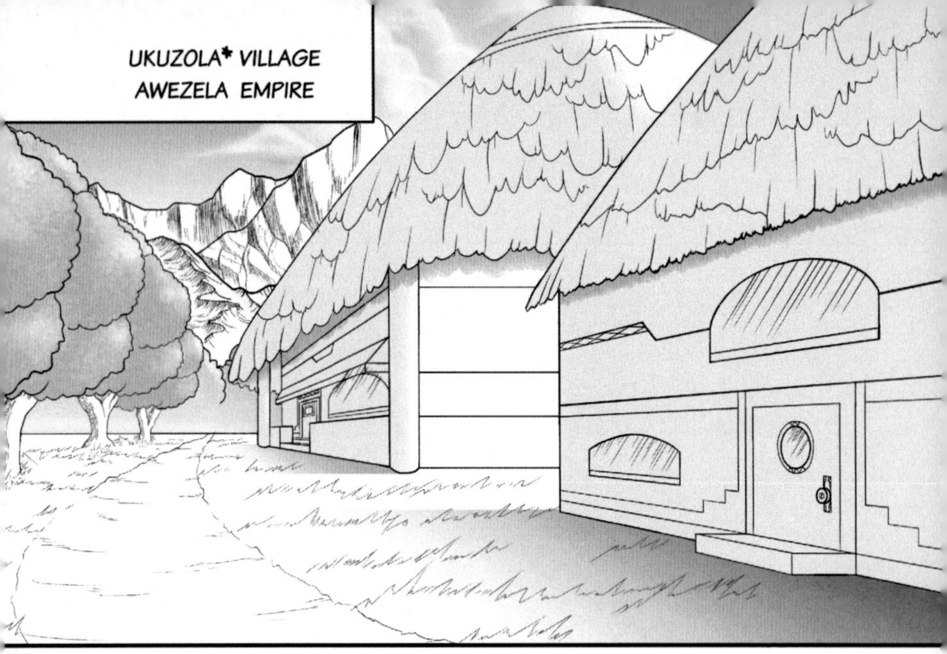
UKUZOLA* VILLAGE
AWEZELA EMPIRE

*UKUZOLA IS THE XHOSA TERM FOR CALM

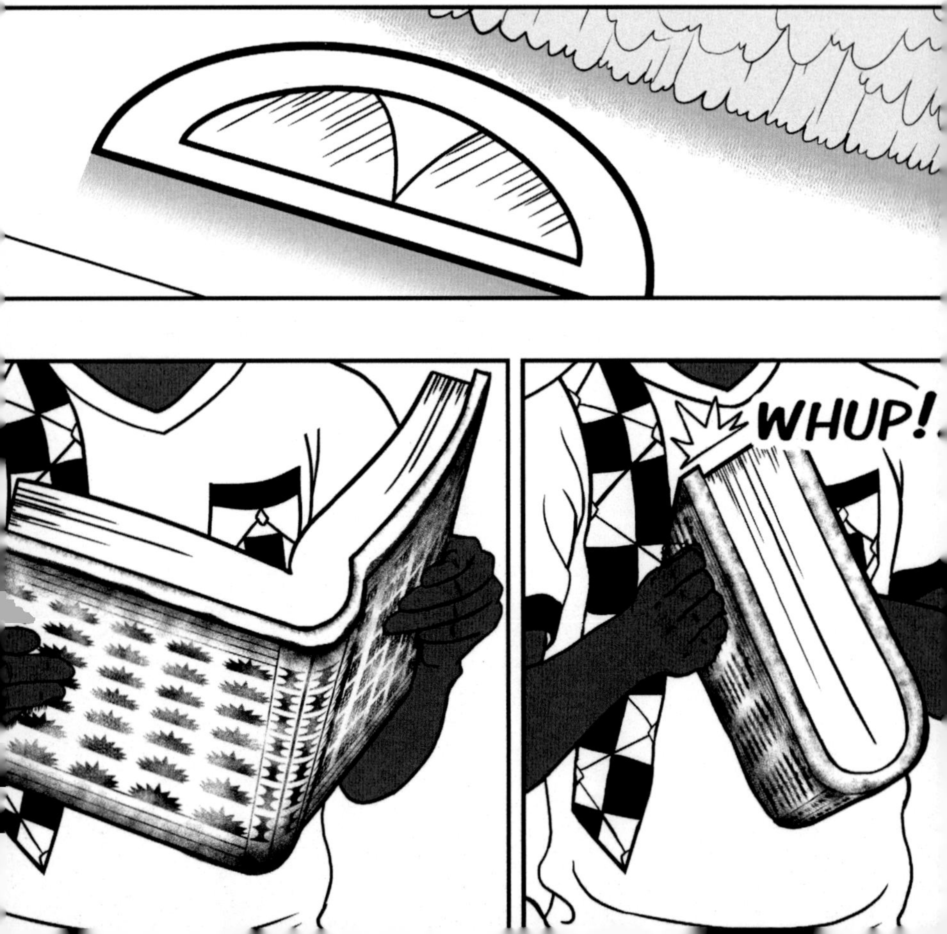
WHUP!

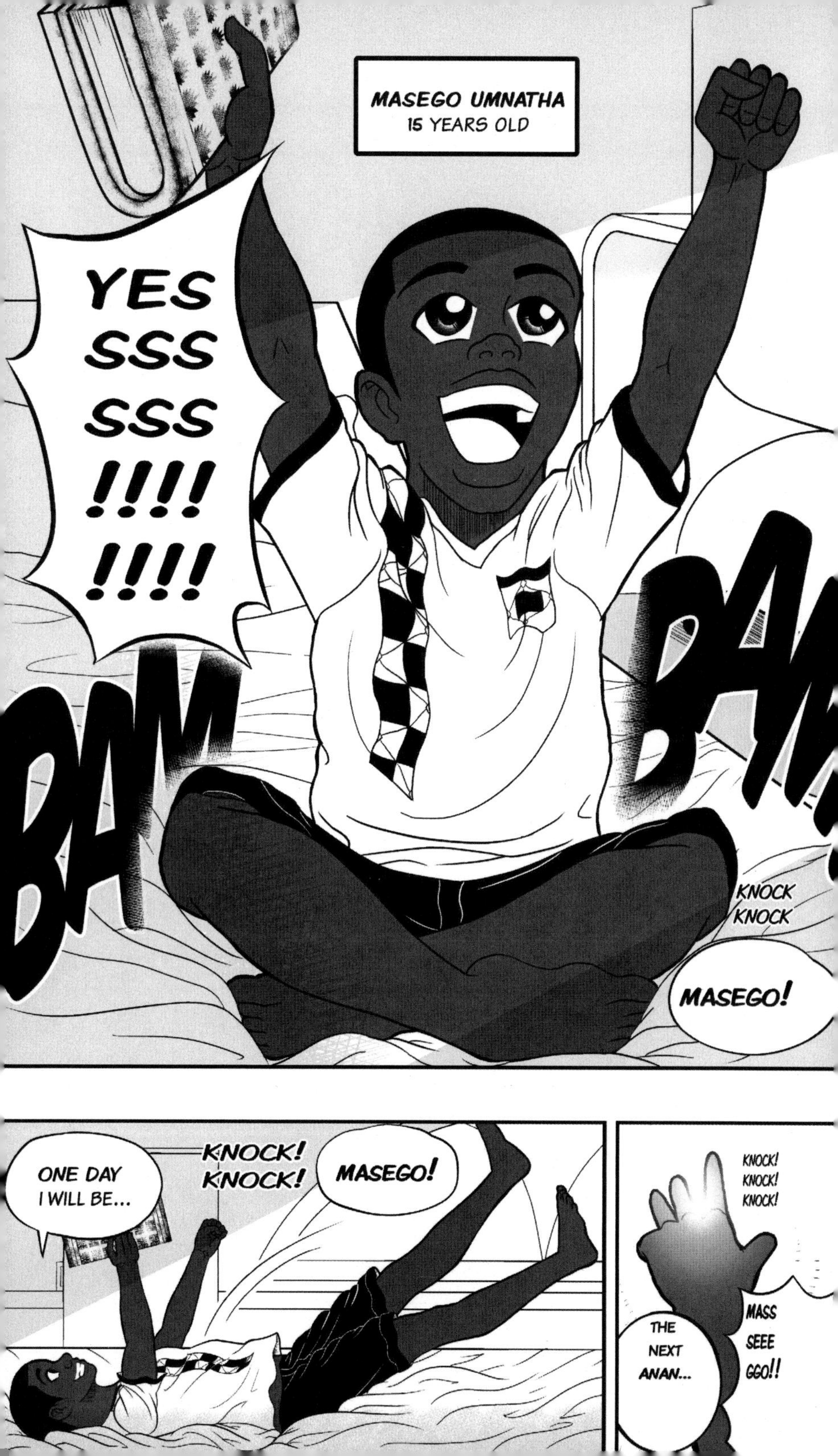
MASEGO UMNATHA
15 YEARS OLD
YES SSS SSS !!!! !!!!
BAM
BAM
KNOCK KNOCK
MASEGO!
ONE DAY I WILL BE...
KNOCK! KNOCK!
MASEGO!
KNOCK! KNOCK! KNOCK!
THE NEXT ANAN...
MASS SEEE GGO!!

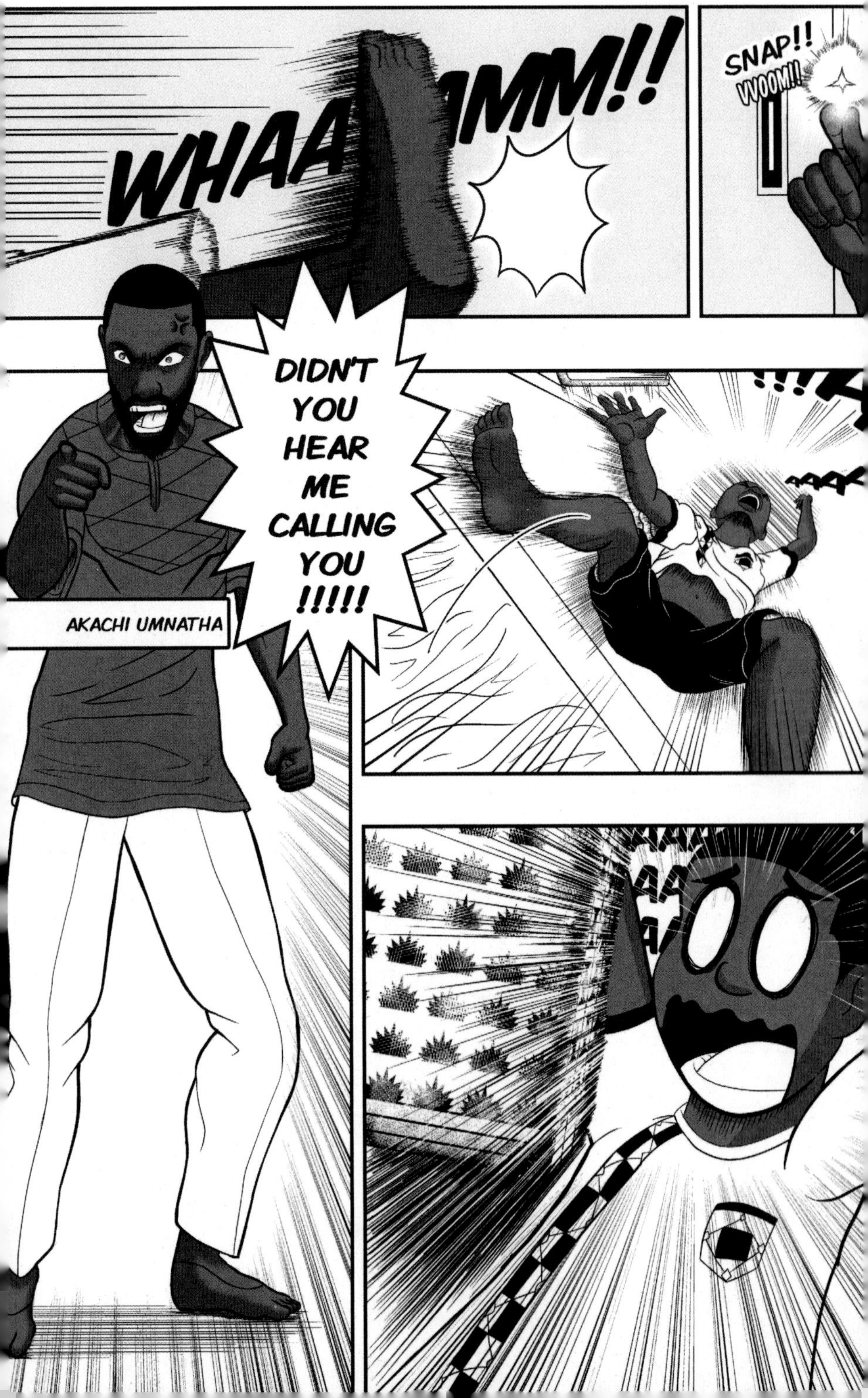
WHAA MMM!!
SNAP!!
VVOOM!!
DIDN'T YOU HEAR ME CALLING YOU !!!!!
AKACHI UMNATHA
!!!

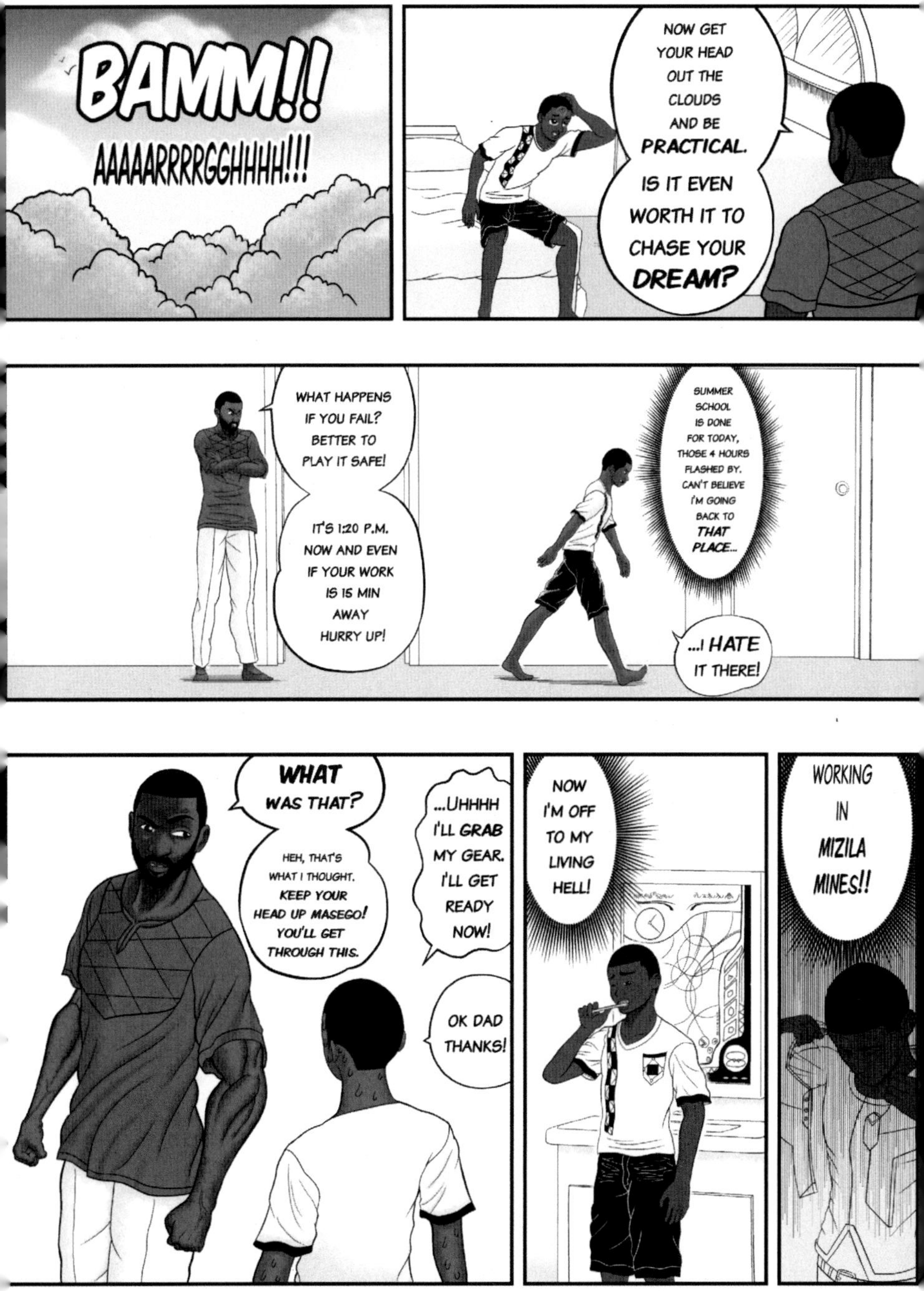
BAMM!!
AAAAARRRRGGHHHH!!!
NOW GET YOUR HEAD OUT THE CLOUDS AND BE PRACTICAL.
IS IT EVEN WORTH IT TO CHASE YOUR DREAM?
WHAT HAPPENS IF YOU FAIL? BETTER TO PLAY IT SAFE!
IT'S 1:20 P.M. NOW AND EVEN IF YOUR WORK IS 15 MIN AWAY HURRY UP!
SUMMER SCHOOL IS DONE FOR TODAY, THOSE 4 HOURS FLASHED BY. CAN'T BELIEVE I'M GOING BACK TO THAT PLACE...
...I HATE IT THERE!
WHAT WAS THAT?
HEH, THAT'S WHAT I THOUGHT. KEEP YOUR HEAD UP MASEGO! YOU'LL GET THROUGH THIS.
...UHHHH I'LL GRAB MY GEAR. I'LL GET READY NOW!
OK DAD THANKS!
NOW I'M OFF TO MY LIVING HELL!
WORKING IN MIZILA MINES!!

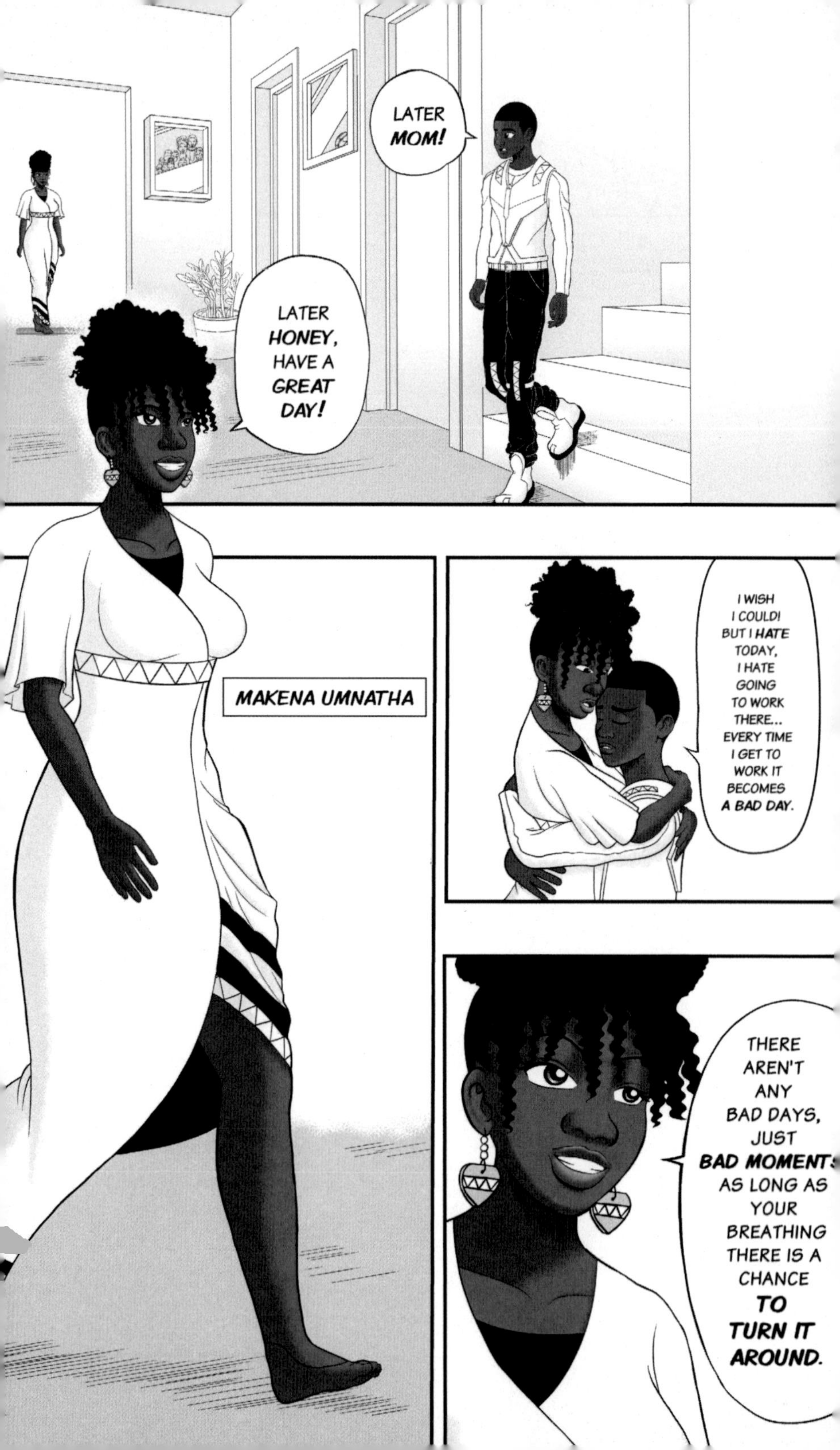
LATER MOM!
LATER HONEY, HAVE A GREAT DAY!
MAKENA UMNATHA
I WISH I COULD! BUT I HATE TODAY, I HATE GOING TO WORK THERE... EVERY TIME I GET TO WORK IT BECOMES A BAD DAY.
THERE AREN'T ANY BAD DAYS, JUST BAD MOMENTS AS LONG AS YOUR BREATHING THERE IS A CHANCE TO TURN IT AROUND.

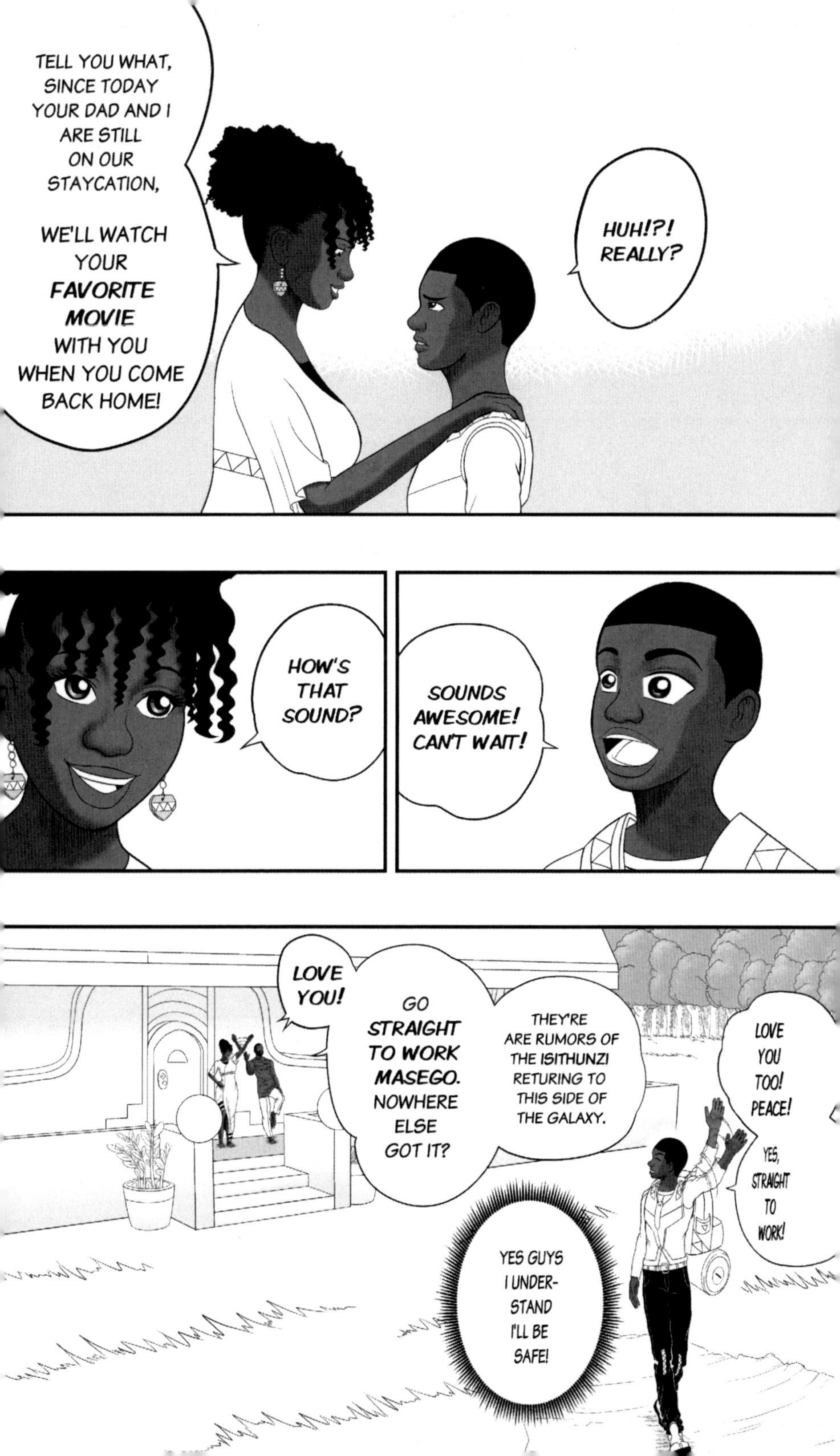
TELL YOU WHAT, SINCE TODAY YOUR DAD AND I ARE STILL ON OUR STAYCATION,
WE'LL WATCH YOUR **FAVORITE MOVIE** WITH YOU WHEN YOU COME BACK HOME!
HUH!?! REALLY?
HOW'S THAT SOUND?
SOUNDS AWESOME! CAN'T WAIT!
LOVE YOU!
GO **STRAIGHT TO WORK MASEGO.** NOWHERE ELSE GOT IT?
THEY'RE ARE RUMORS OF THE ISITHUNZI RETURING TO THIS SIDE OF THE GALAXY.
LOVE YOU TOO! PEACE!
YES, STRAIGHT TO WORK!
YES GUYS I UNDER-STAND I'LL BE SAFE!

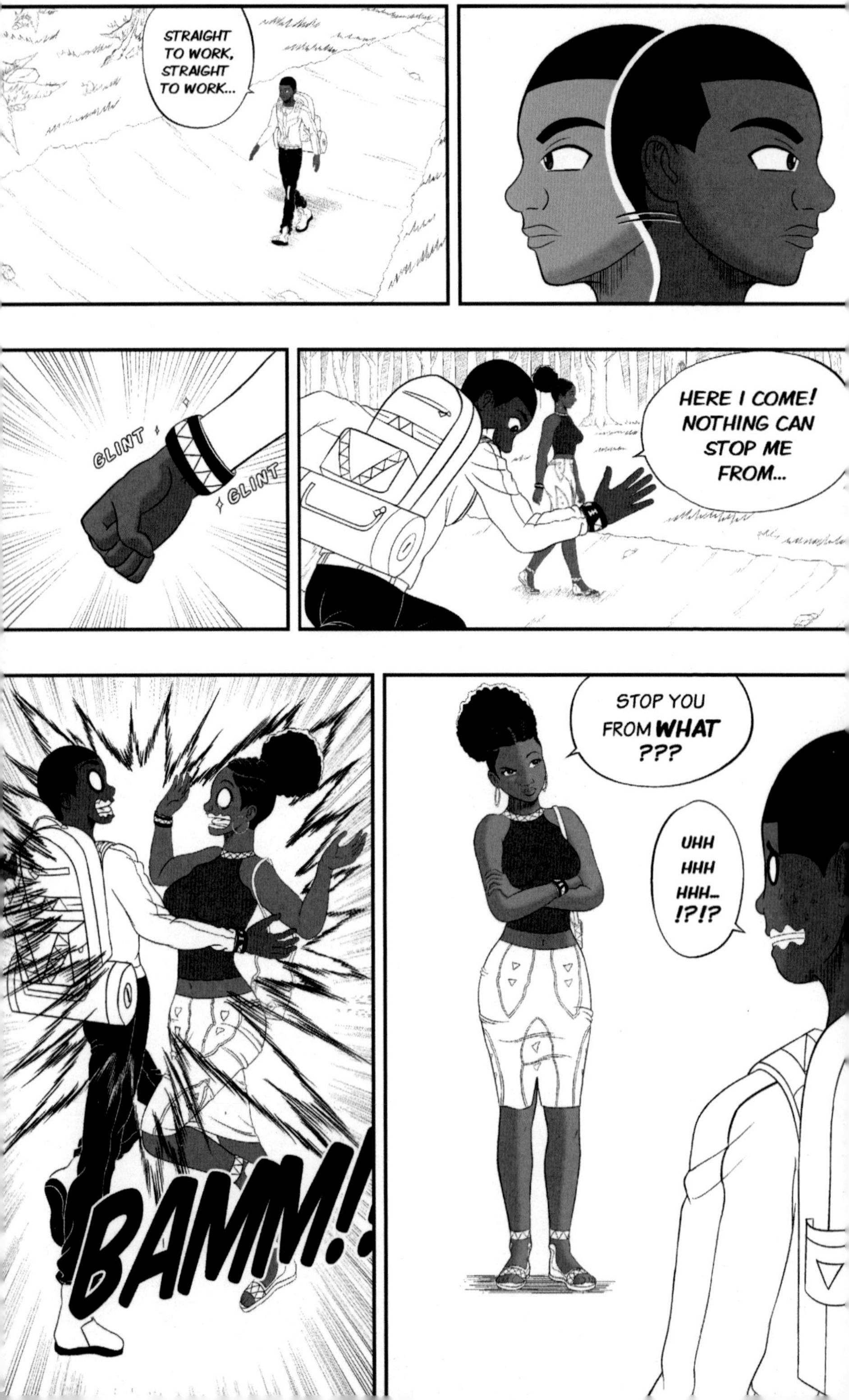
STRAIGHT TO WORK, STRAIGHT TO WORK...
GLINT
GLINT
HERE I COME! NOTHING CAN STOP ME FROM...
BAMM!!
STOP YOU FROM WHAT ???
UHH HHH HHH... !?!?

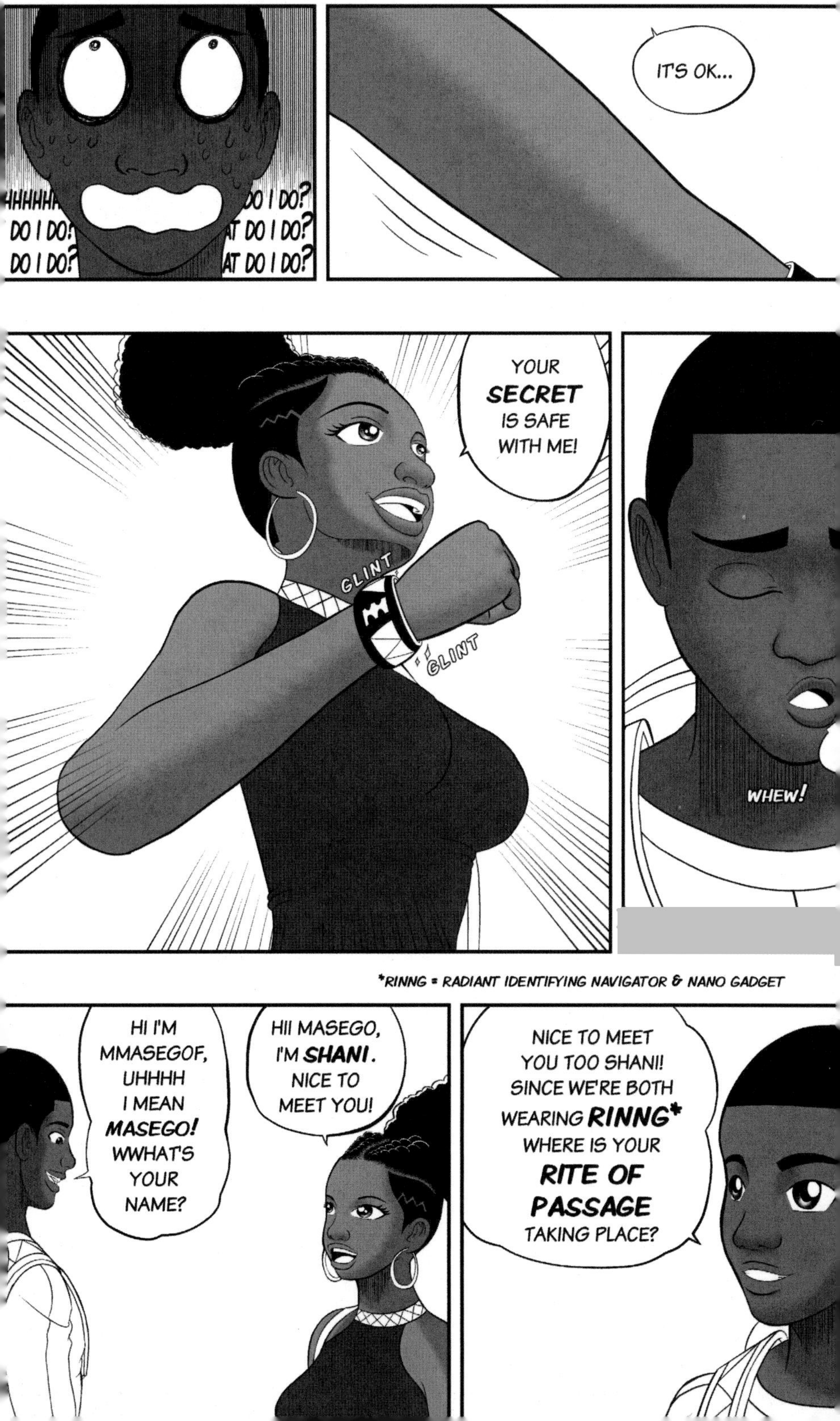
HHHHH
DO I DO!
DO I DO?
DO I DO?
OO I DO?
AT DO I DO?
AT DO I DO?
IT'S OK...
YOUR SECRET IS SAFE WITH ME!
GLINT
GLINT
WHEW!
*RINNG = RADIANT IDENTIFYING NAVIGATOR & NANO GADGET
HI I'M MMASEGOF, UHHHH I MEAN MASEGO! WWHAT'S YOUR NAME?
HII MASEGO, I'M SHANI. NICE TO MEET YOU!
NICE TO MEET YOU TOO SHANI! SINCE WE'RE BOTH WEARING RINNG* WHERE IS YOUR RITE OF PASSAGE TAKING PLACE?

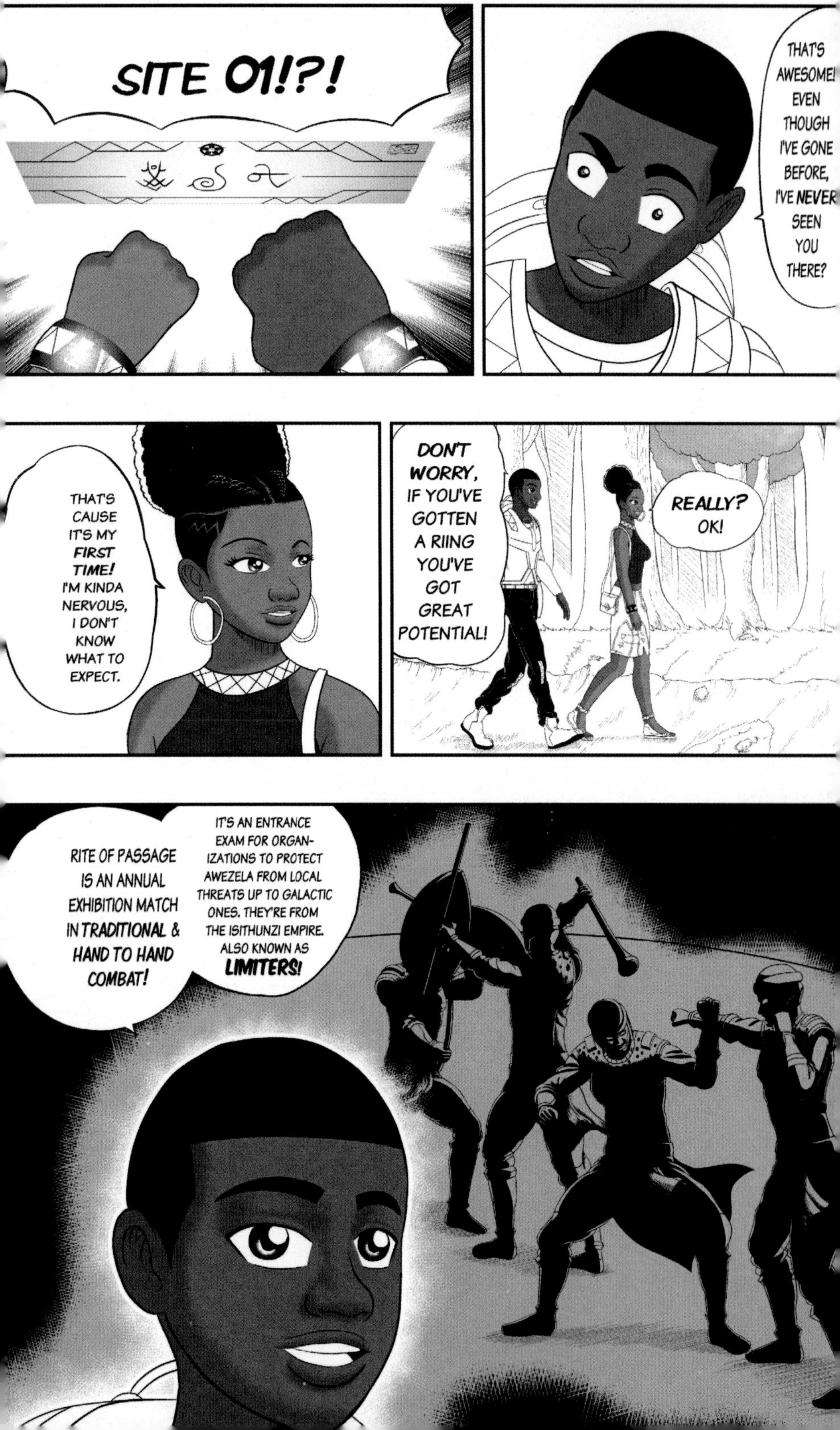
SITE 01!?!
THAT'S AWESOME! EVEN THOUGH I'VE GONE BEFORE, I'VE NEVER SEEN YOU THERE?
THAT'S CAUSE IT'S MY FIRST TIME! I'M KINDA NERVOUS, I DON'T KNOW WHAT TO EXPECT.
DON'T WORRY, IF YOU'VE GOTTEN A RIING YOU'VE GOT GREAT POTENTIAL!
REALLY? OK!
RITE OF PASSAGE IS AN ANNUAL EXHIBITION MATCH IN TRADITIONAL & HAND TO HAND COMBAT!
IT'S AN ENTRANCE EXAM FOR ORGAN-IZATIONS TO PROTECT AWEZELA FROM LOCAL THREATS UP TO GALACTIC ONES. THEY'RE FROM THE ISITHUNZI EMPIRE. ALSO KNOWN AS LIMITERS!

ONCE YOU PASS, YOU HAVE **2** CHOICES!

OK, WHAT ARE THEY?

THE FIRST CHOICE IS THE NATIONAL EDUCATION BREAKTHROUGH UNLIMITED LEADERSHIP ACADEMY OR **NEBULA.**

IT WAS FORMED WITHIN THE LAST 100 YEARS TO PREPARE THE BEST OF THE BEST FOR ALL THAT STAAR HAS TO OFFER!

IT'S ONLY AVAILABLE FOR AGES 10–15 SO I AGED OUT. THIS IS... UHH... ACTUALLY **MY 5TH ATTEMPT.**

WOW THAT'S **A LOT!** YOU MUST REALLY WANT TO **GET IN!**

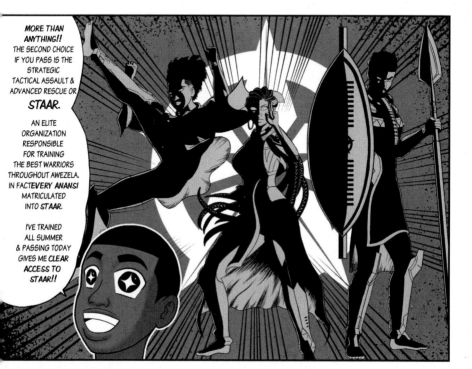

MORE THAN ANYTHING!! THE SECOND CHOICE IF YOU PASS IS THE STRATEGIC TACTICAL ASSAULT & ADVANCED RESCUE OR **STAAR.**

AN ELITE ORGANIZATION RESPONSIBLE FOR TRAINING THE BEST WARRIORS THROUGHOUT AWEZELA. IN FACT **EVERY ANANSI** MATRICULATED INTO **STAAR.**

I'VE TRAINED ALL SUMMER & PASSING TODAY GIVES ME **CLEAR ACCESS TO STAAR!!**

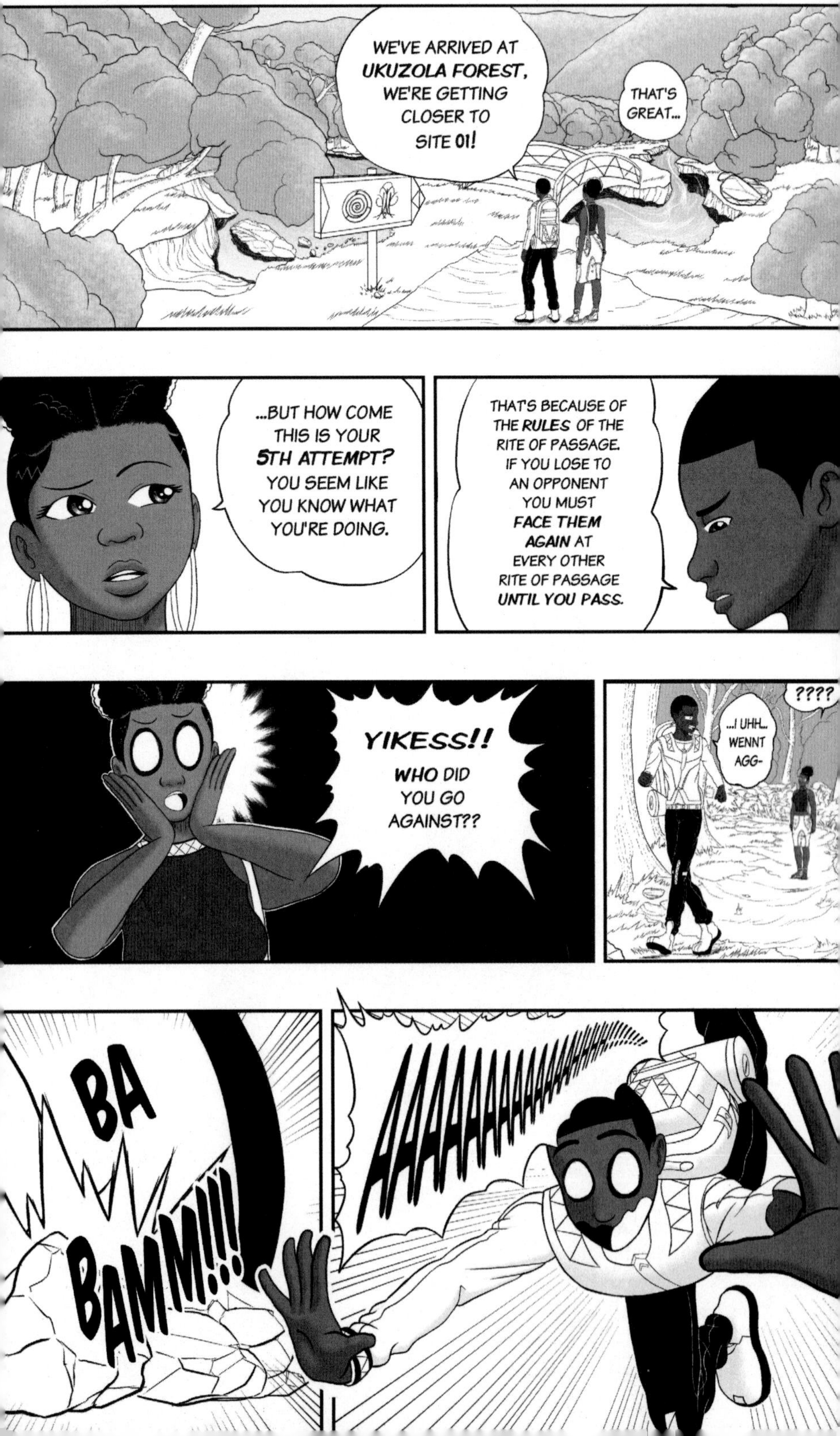
WE'VE ARRIVED AT UKUZOLA FOREST, WE'RE GETTING CLOSER TO SITE 01!
THAT'S GREAT...
...BUT HOW COME THIS IS YOUR 5TH ATTEMPT? YOU SEEM LIKE YOU KNOW WHAT YOU'RE DOING.
THAT'S BECAUSE OF THE RULES OF THE RITE OF PASSAGE. IF YOU LOSE TO AN OPPONENT YOU MUST FACE THEM AGAIN AT EVERY OTHER RITE OF PASSAGE UNTIL YOU PASS.
YIKESS!! WHO DID YOU GO AGAINST??
...I UHH... WENNT AGG-
????
BA BAMM!!!
AAAAAAAAAAAHHHHH!!!

SINCE I FAILED **4** YEARS AGO AT THE RITE OF PASSAGE MY OPPONENT HAS BEEN AN ***ARROGANT*** & ***PROUD WARRIOR...***

GLARE!!

THE PUGNACIOUS ***BOIPELO ISIBINDI.***

FOR EVERY L I TOOK I ***GRINDED*** HARDER!

I AM DOING ALL THIS TO FULFILL A PROMISE I MADE TO A CLOSE FAMILY MEMBER...

TODAY'S THE DAY I GET THE W, THAT I ***WIPE*** THAT SMUG LOOK OFF HIS ANNOYING FACE!

YOU GOT THIS!

TODAY'S THE DAY I ***MOVE FORWARD*** TOWARDS ***MY DREAM.***

OK, I'LL BE ROOTING FOR YOU.

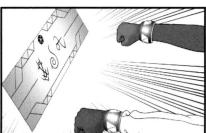

OK SHANI, IT'S JUST BEYOND THESE BUSHES...

RUSTLE

RUSTLE

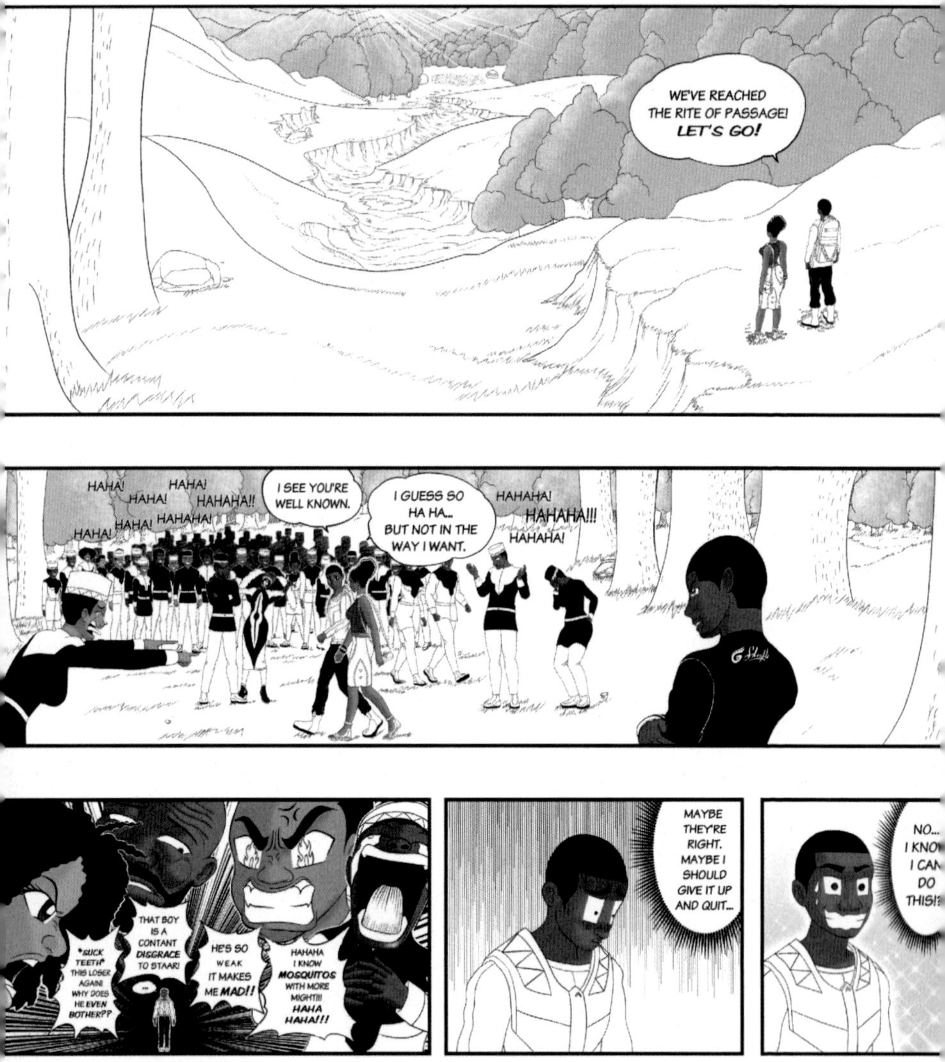
WE'VE REACHED THE RITE OF PASSAGE! LET'S GO!
HAHA! HAHA! HAHA! HAHAHA!! HAHA! HAHA! HAHAHA!
I SEE YOU'RE WELL KNOWN.
I GUESS SO HA HA... BUT NOT IN THE WAY I WANT.
HAHAHA! HAHAHA!!! HAHAHA!
SUCK TEETH THIS LOSER AGAIN! WHY DOES HE EVEN BOTHER??
THAT BOY IS A CONTANT DISGRACE TO STAAR!
...
HE'S SO WEAK IT MAKES ME MAD!!
HAHAHA I KNOW MOSQUITOS WITH MORE MIGHT!!! HAHA HAHA!!!
MAYBE THEY'RE RIGHT. MAYBE I SHOULD GIVE IT UP AND QUIT...
NO... I KNOW I CAN DO THIS!?

*EISHI! IS A KHOI TERM FOR EXPRESSING EXCLAMATION FROM SUPRISE OR SHOCK.

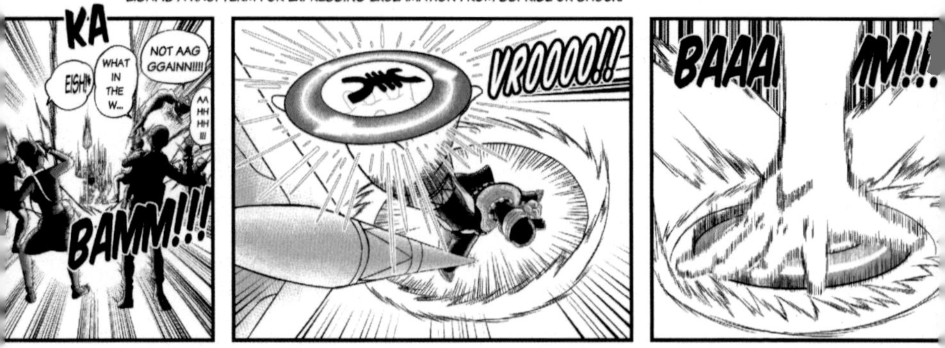
KA
EISHI!*
WHAT IN THE W...
NOT AAG GGAINN!!!!
AAHHHH!!!
BAMM!!!
VROOOO!!
BAAAM!!!

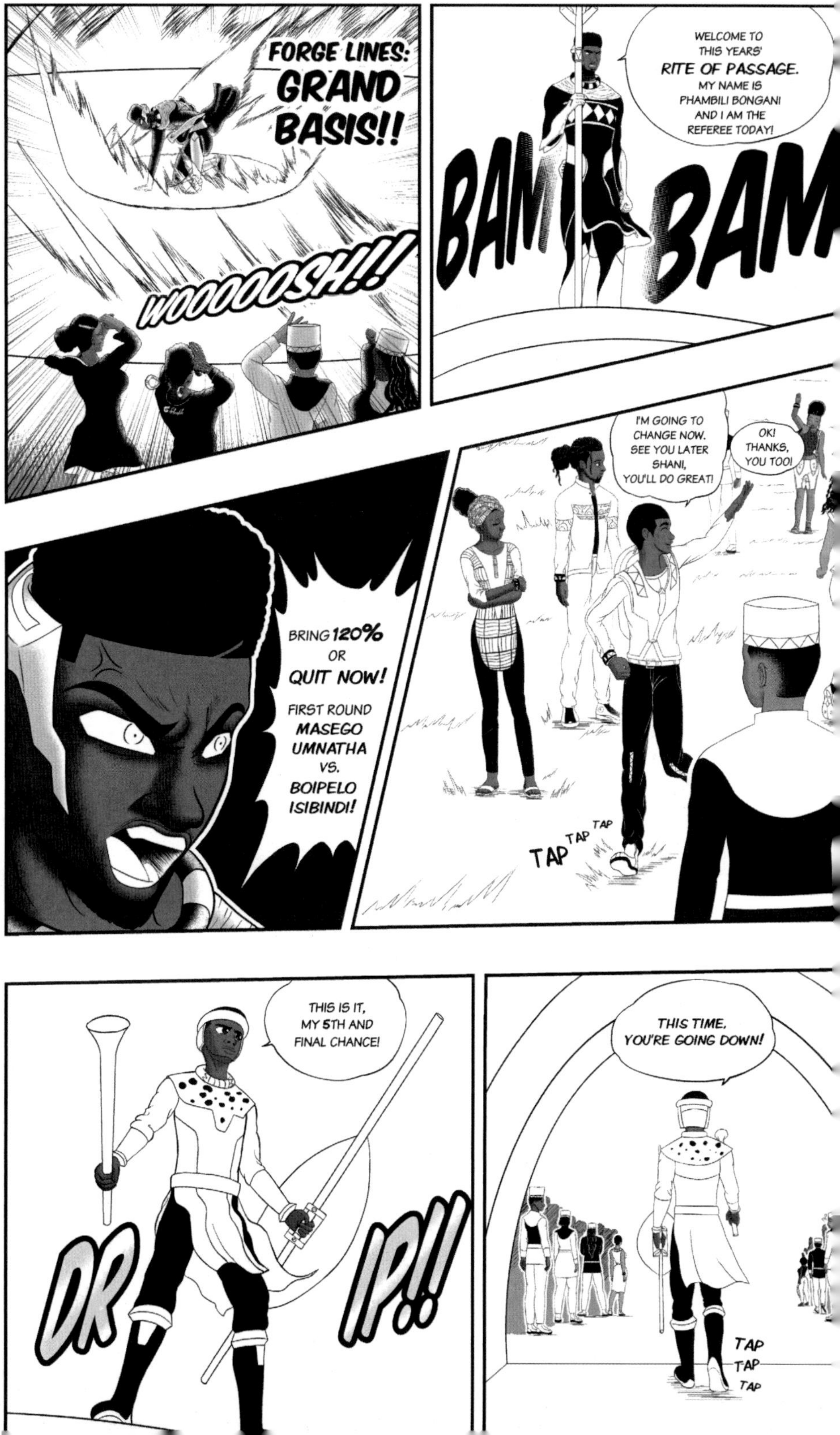
FORGE LINES: GRAND BASIS!!
WOOOOOOSH!!
WELCOME TO THIS YEARS' RITE OF PASSAGE. MY NAME IS PHAMBILI BONGANI AND I AM THE REFEREE TODAY!
BAM BAM
BRING 120% OR QUIT NOW!
FIRST ROUND MASEGO UMNATHA VS. BOIPELO ISIBINDI!
I'M GOING TO CHANGE NOW. SEE YOU LATER SHANI, YOU'LL DO GREAT!
OK! THANKS, YOU TOO!
TAP TAP TAP
THIS IS IT, MY 5TH AND FINAL CHANCE!
DR IP!!
THIS TIME, YOU'RE GOING DOWN!
TAP TAP TAP

THERE HE GOES...AGAIN
WHEN WILL HE LEARN.
WHO KNOWS.
YOUR WINNING STREAK ENDS HERE!
YOU'RE PATHETIC! UNWORTHY OF NEBULA, STAAR AND YOU'VE LOST TO ME 4 YEARS IN A ROW. WHAT MAKES TODAY DIFFERENT?
BOIPELO ISIBINDI
STOP CAPPIN!!

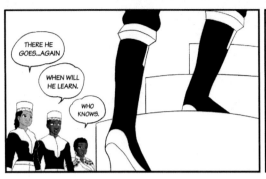

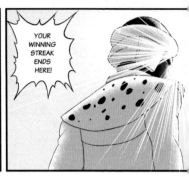

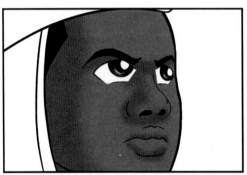

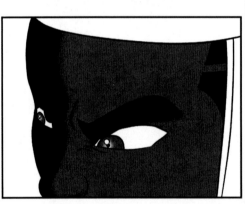

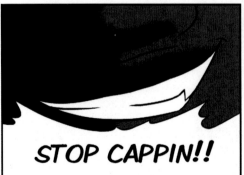

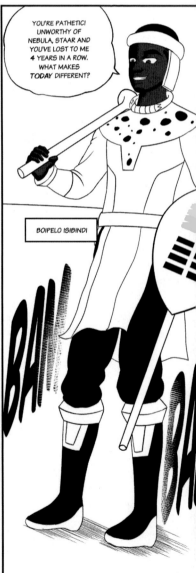

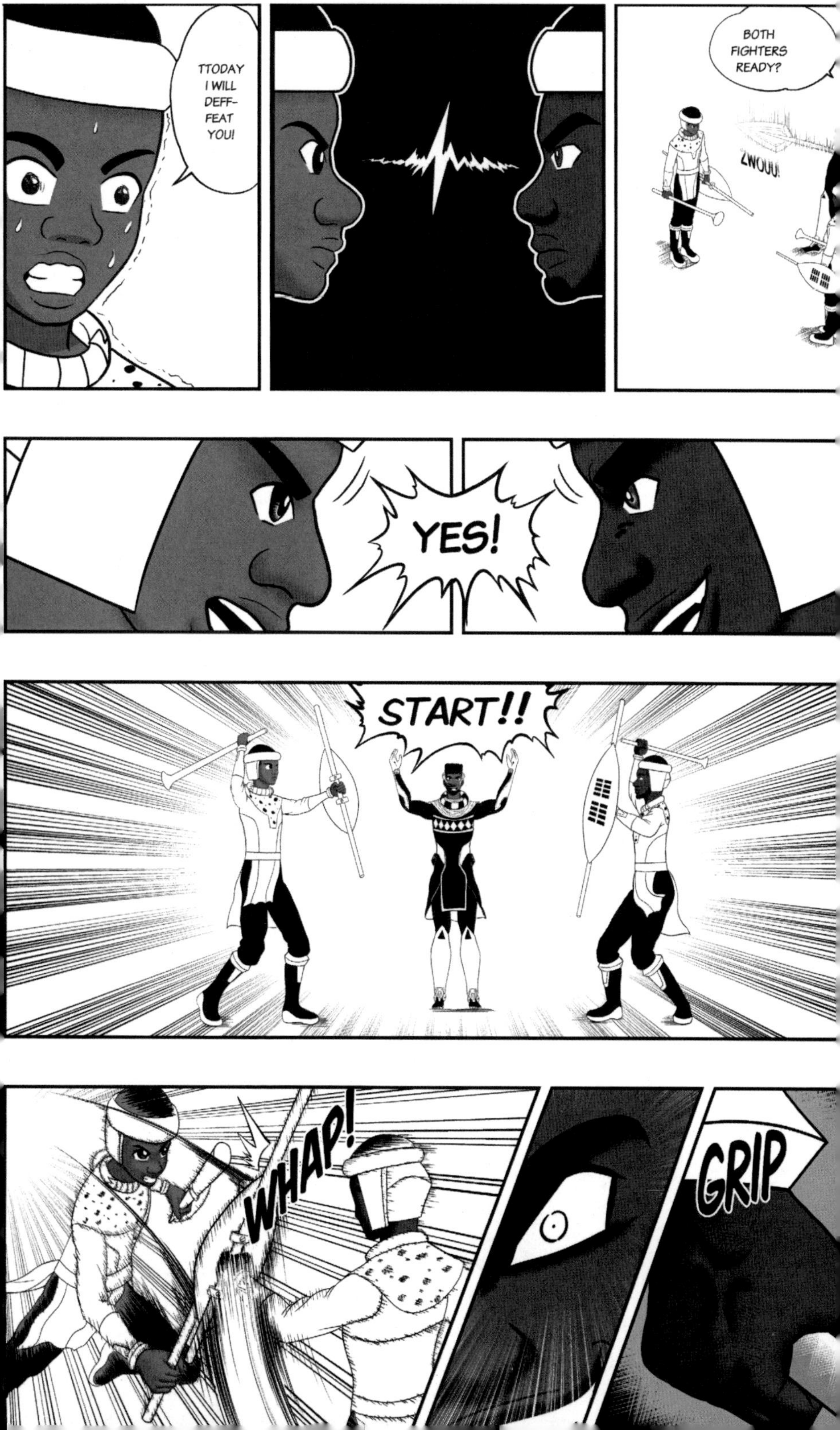
TTODAY I WILL DEFF-FEAT YOU!
BOTH FIGHTERS READY?
ZWOUU!
YES!
START!!
WHAP!
GRIP

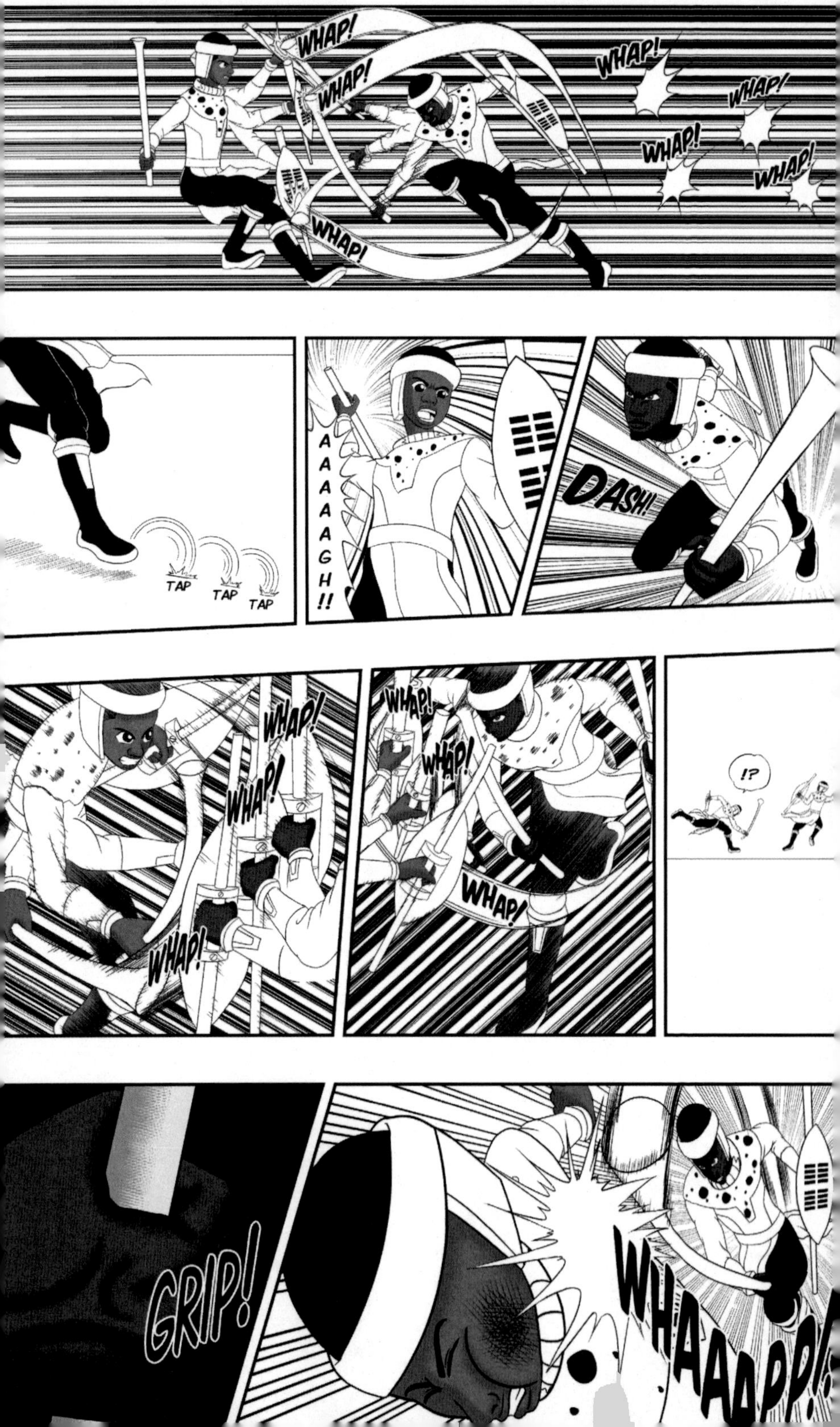
WHAP!
WHAP!
WHAP!
WHAP!
WHAP!
WHAP!
WHAP!
WHAP!
TAP
TAP
TAP
AAAAAAAGH!!
DASH!
WHAP!
WHAP!
WHAP!
WHAP!
WHAP!
WHAP!
!?
GRIP!
WHAAAP!!

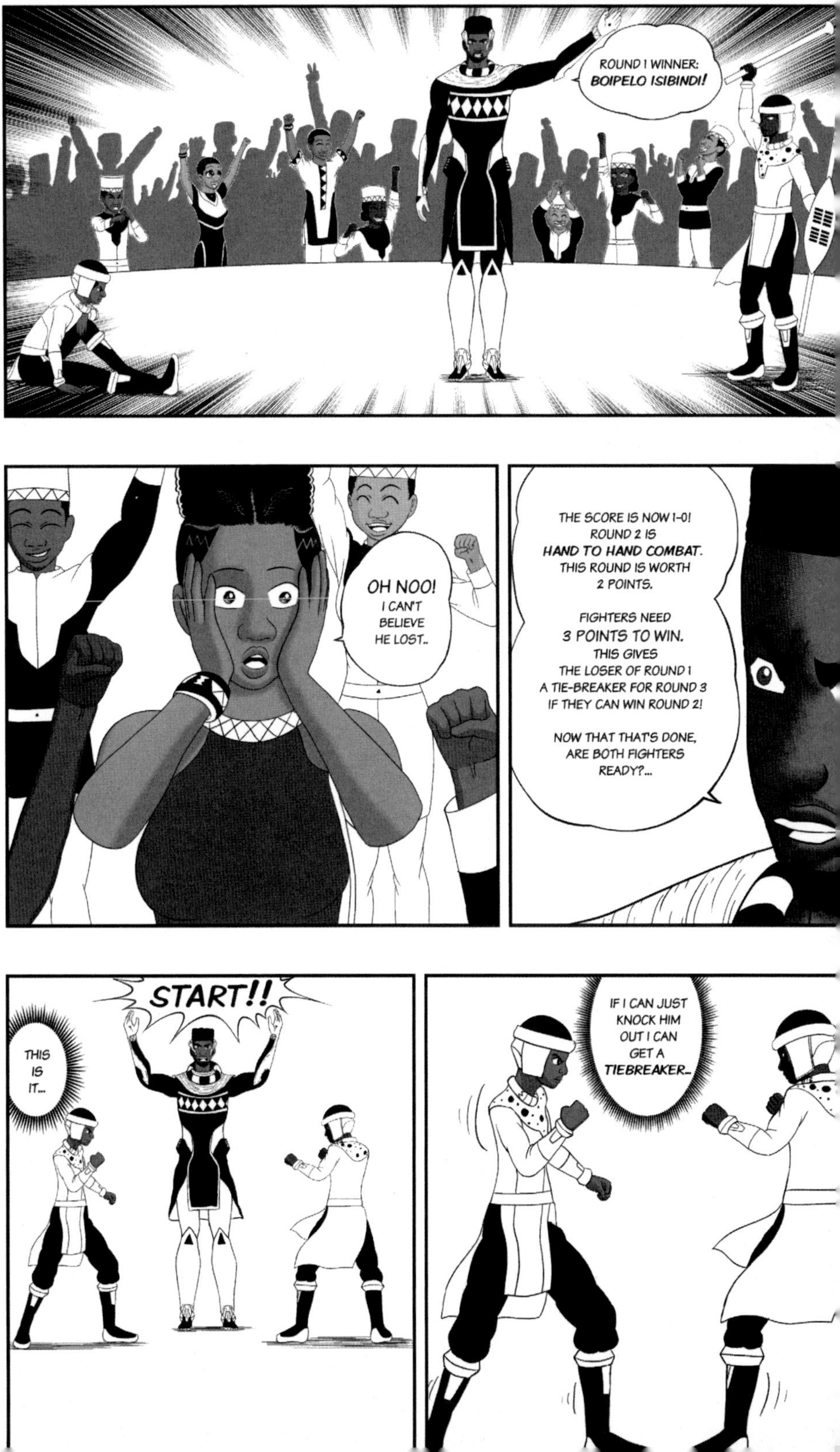
ROUND 1 WINNER: BOIPELO ISIBINDI!
OH NOO! I CAN'T BELIEVE HE LOST..
THE SCORE IS NOW 1-0! ROUND 2 IS HAND TO HAND COMBAT. THIS ROUND IS WORTH 2 POINTS.
FIGHTERS NEED 3 POINTS TO WIN. THIS GIVES THE LOSER OF ROUND 1 A TIE-BREAKER FOR ROUND 3 IF THEY CAN WIN ROUND 2!
NOW THAT THAT'S DONE, ARE BOTH FIGHTERS READY?...
THIS IS IT...
START!!
IF I CAN JUST KNOCK HIM OUT I CAN GET A TIEBREAKER...

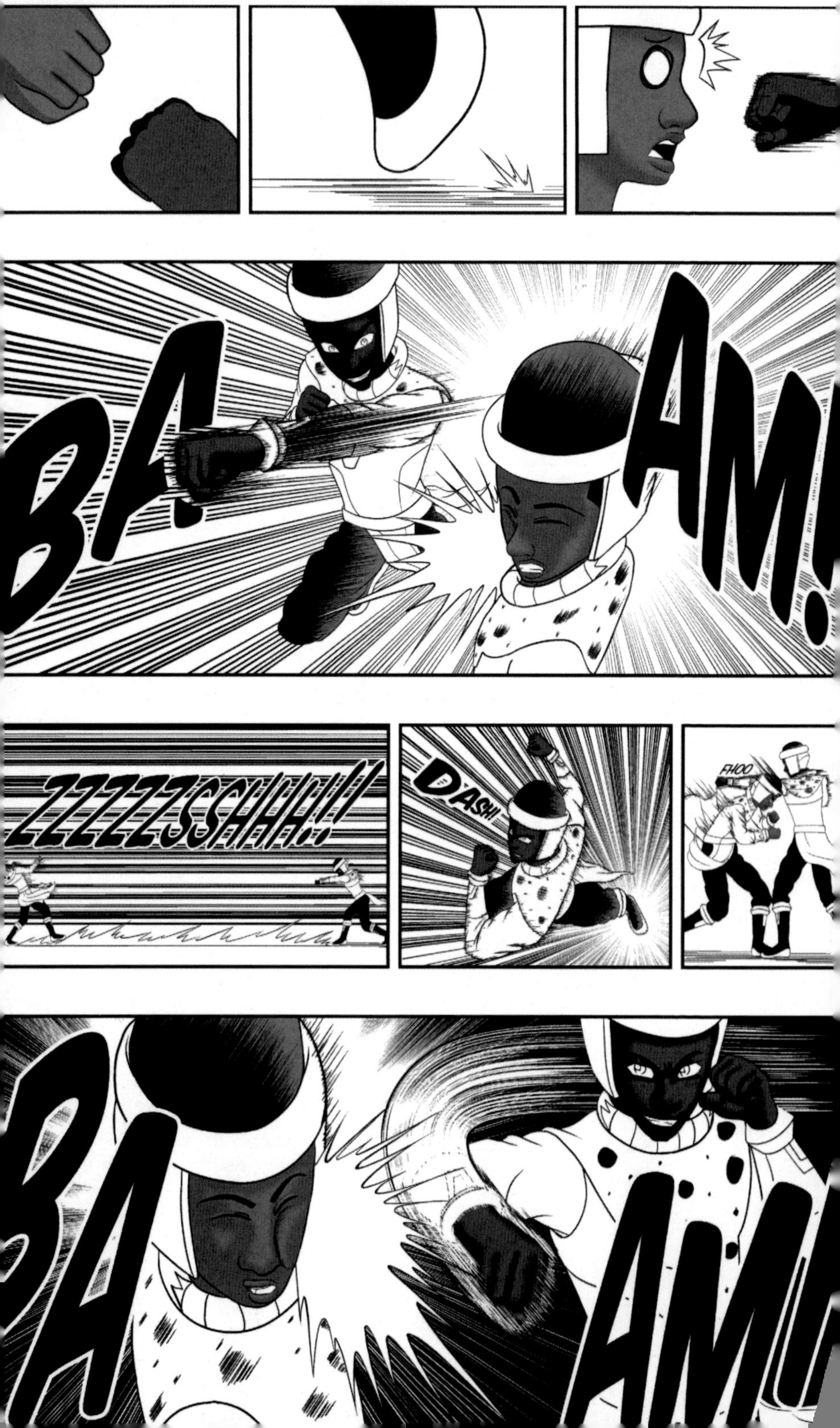
BAAM!!
ZZZZZZSSHHH!!
DASH!!
FHOO
BAAM!!

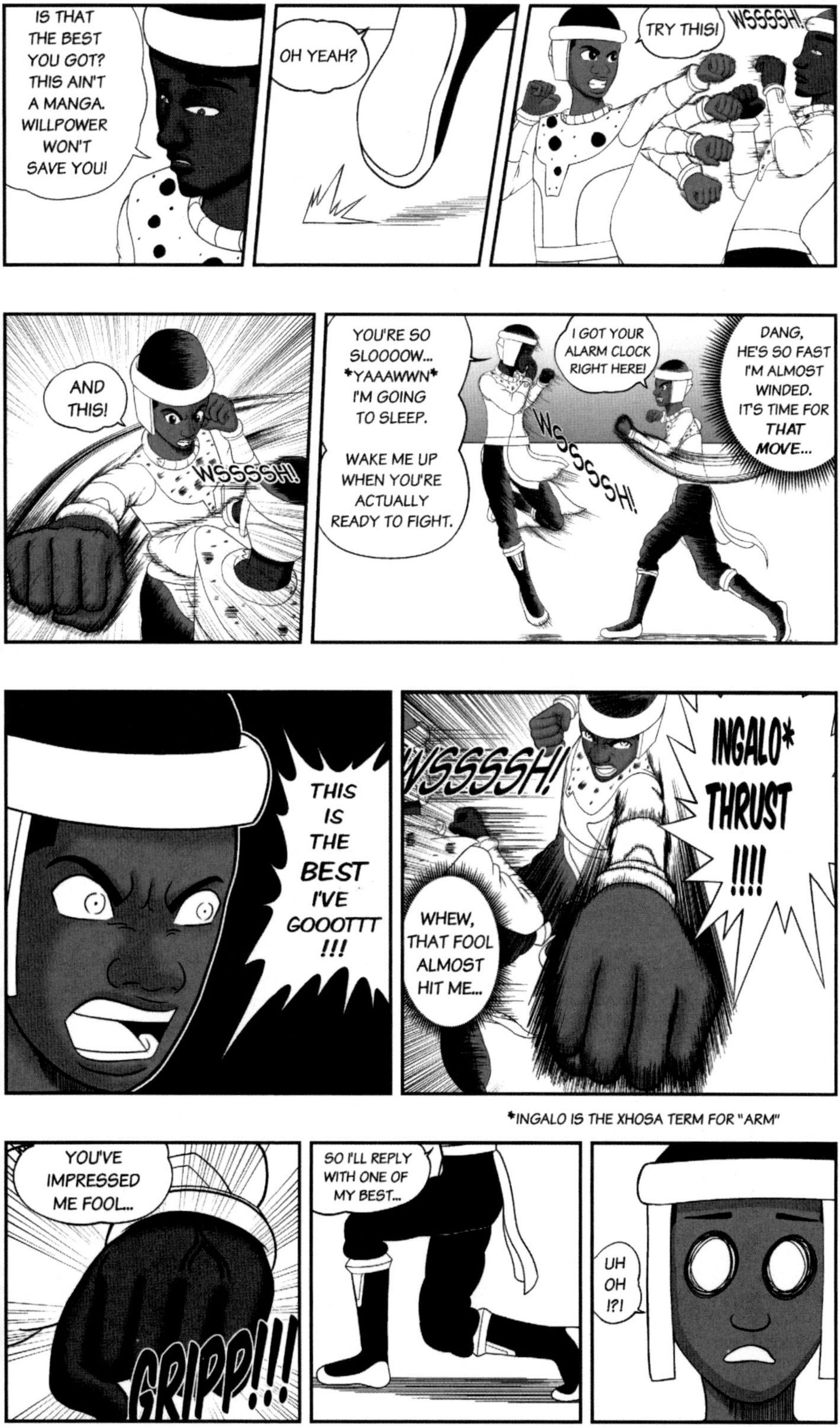
IS THAT THE BEST YOU GOT? THIS AIN'T A MANGA. WILLPOWER WON'T SAVE YOU!
OH YEAH?
TRY THIS!
WSSSSH!
AND THIS!
WSSSSH!
YOU'RE SO SLOOOOW... *YAAAWWN* I'M GOING TO SLEEP.
WAKE ME UP WHEN YOU'RE ACTUALLY READY TO FIGHT.
I GOT YOUR ALARM CLOCK RIGHT HERE!
WSSSSSH!
DANG, HE'S SO FAST I'M ALMOST WINDED. IT'S TIME FOR THAT MOVE...
THIS IS THE BEST I'VE GOOOTTT !!!
WSSSSH!
INGALO* THRUST !!!!
WHEW, THAT FOOL ALMOST HIT ME...
*INGALO IS THE XHOSA TERM FOR "ARM"
YOU'VE IMPRESSED ME FOOL...
GRIPP!!!
SO I'LL REPLY WITH ONE OF MY BEST...
UH OH !?!

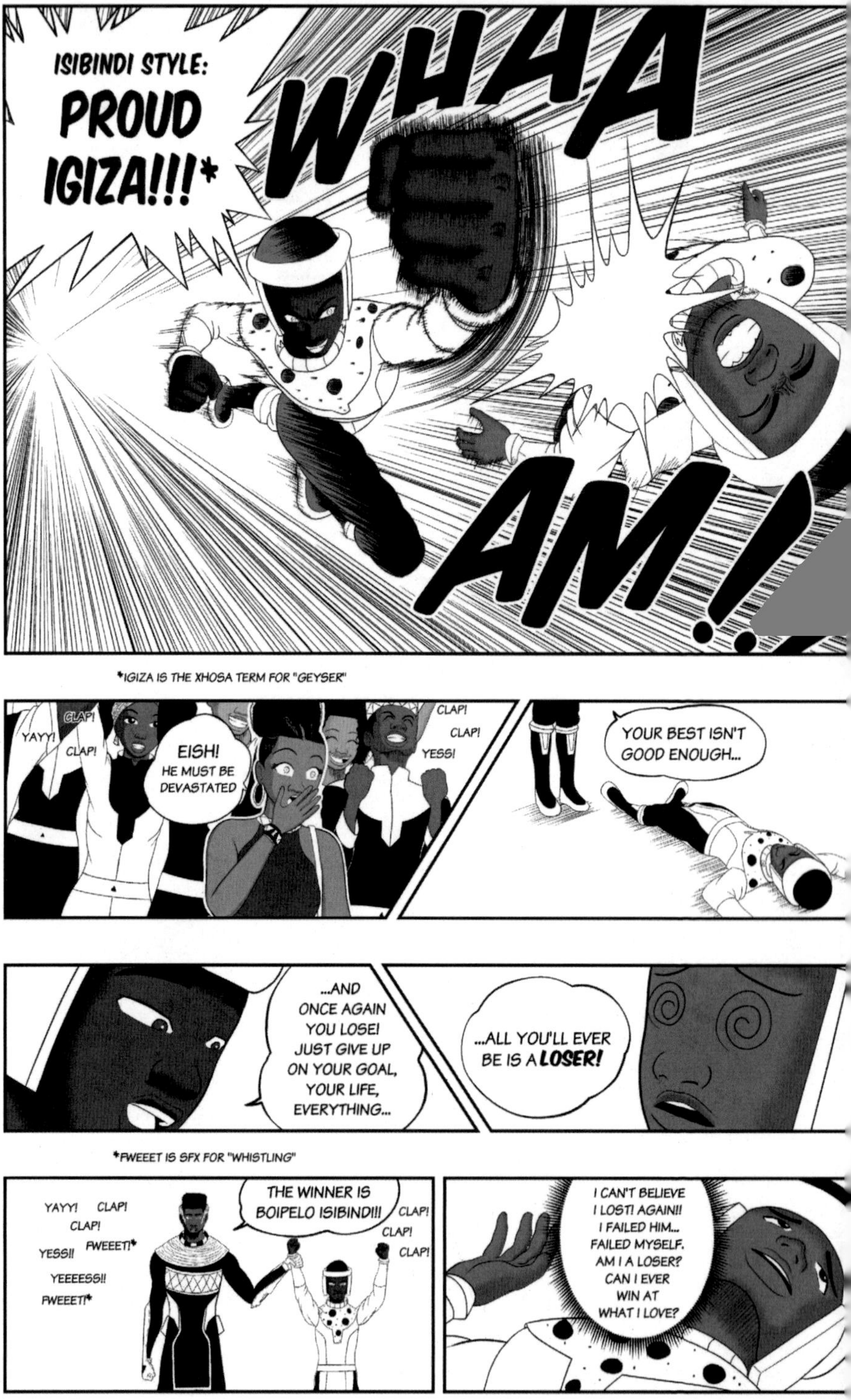
ISIBINDI STYLE: PROUD IGIZA!!!*
WHAA
AM!!
*IGIZA IS THE XHOSA TERM FOR "GEYSER"
CLAP!
YAYY!
CLAP!
EISH! HE MUST BE DEVASTATED
CLAP!
CLAP!
YESS!
YOUR BEST ISN'T GOOD ENOUGH...
...AND ONCE AGAIN YOU LOSE! JUST GIVE UP ON YOUR GOAL, YOUR LIFE, EVERYTHING...
...ALL YOU'LL EVER BE IS A LOSER!
*FWEEET IS SFX FOR "WHISTLING"
YAYY! CLAP!
CLAP!
YESS!! FWEEET!*
YEEEESS!!
FWEEET!*
THE WINNER IS BOIPELO ISIBINDI!!!
CLAP!
CLAP!
CLAP!
I CAN'T BELIEVE I LOST! AGAIN!! I FAILED HIM... FAILED MYSELF. AM I A LOSER? CAN I EVER WIN AT WHAT I LOVE?

THAT FIGHT FELT SOOO LONG, HAD TO BE AT LEAST 2 HOURS OR MORE.

1:42 PM!

THE FIGHT ONLY LASTED 2 MINUTES?!? DARN ITT!!!!

NEXT MATCH, JABULANI IANKILE VS...

HUH, THIS REMINDS ME OF ALL THE YEARS BEFORE...

YEAR 1

YEAR 2

YEAR 3

YEAR 4

...START!

WELL... BACK TO WORK, I GUESS

AFTER TAKING THAT L... ANOTHER REMATCH TODAY ISN'T WORTH IT. LET ME JUST CHANGE BACK INTO MY WORK CLOTHES.

HMM.. ACTUALLY, WHAT TIME IS IT NOW!

WHATTT??! IT'S 1:49 P.M. MY SHIFT AT THE MINES STARTS IN LESS THAT 12 MINUTES!

CRAP, I GOTTA GO NOWW!!! I'M OUT!!

HUH!
HUH!
WHEEZE!

I...MADE IT... THAT WAS CRAZY. I'LL JUST ENTER AND GET TO WORK. I'M SURE NO ONE WILL NOTICE ME.

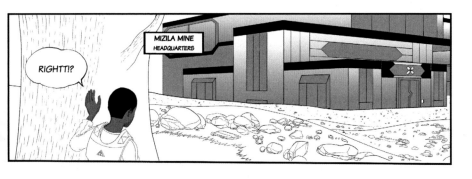

RIGHTT!?

MIZILA MINE
HEADQUARTERS

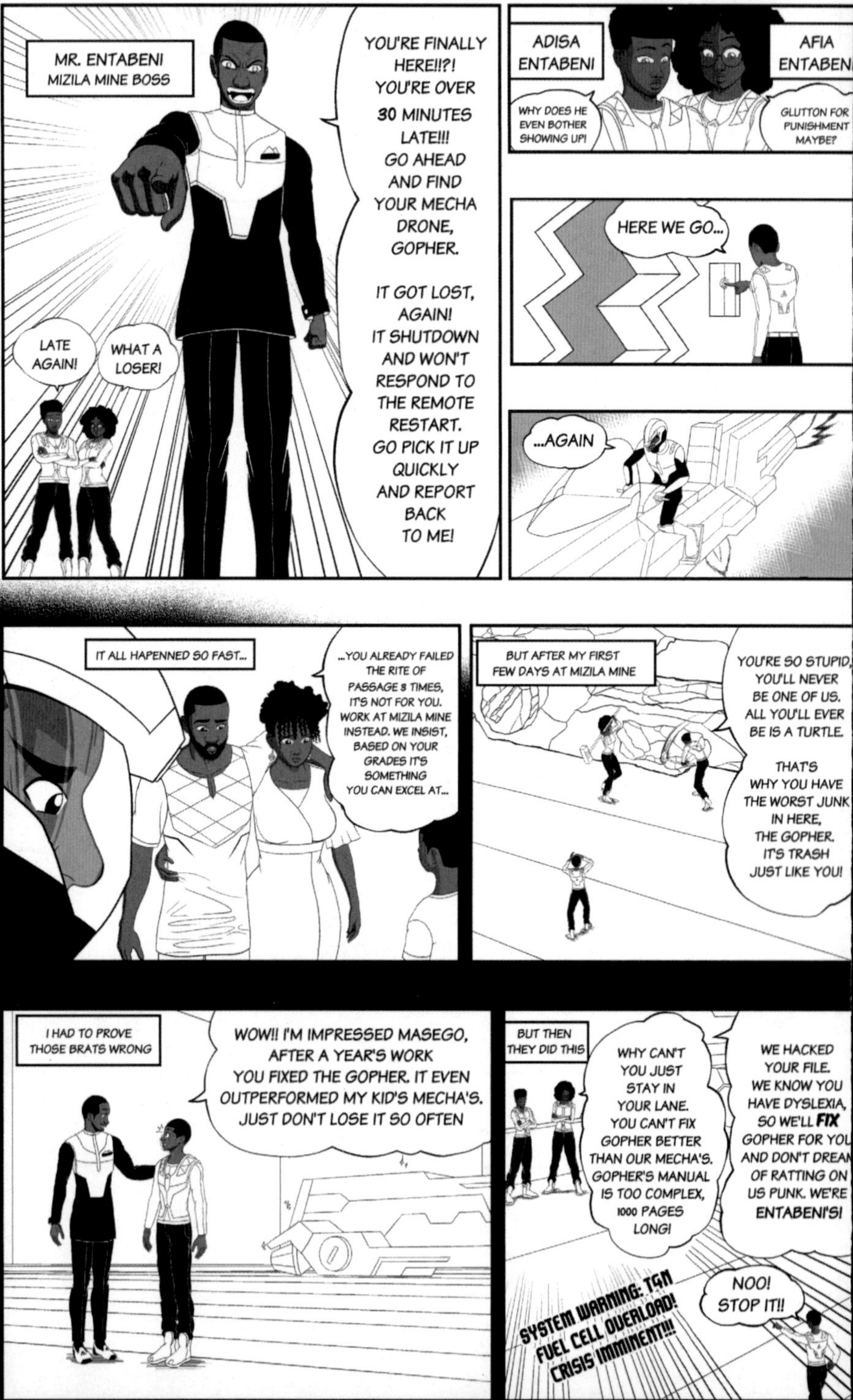

MR. ENTABENI
MIZILA MINE BOSS
YOU'RE FINALLY HERE!!?! YOU'RE OVER 30 MINUTES LATE!!! GO AHEAD AND FIND YOUR MECHA DRONE, GOPHER.
IT GOT LOST, AGAIN! IT SHUTDOWN AND WON'T RESPOND TO THE REMOTE RESTART. GO PICK IT UP QUICKLY AND REPORT BACK TO ME!
LATE AGAIN!
WHAT A LOSER!
ADISA ENTABENI
AFIA ENTABENI
WHY DOES HE EVEN BOTHER SHOWING UP!
GLUTTON FOR PUNISHMENT MAYBE?
HERE WE GO...
...AGAIN
IT ALL HAPENNED SO FAST...
...YOU ALREADY FAILED THE RITE OF PASSAGE 3 TIMES, IT'S NOT FOR YOU. WORK AT MIZILA MINE INSTEAD. WE INSIST, BASED ON YOUR GRADES IT'S SOMETHING YOU CAN EXCEL AT...
BUT AFTER MY FIRST FEW DAYS AT MIZILA MINE
YOU'RE SO STUPID, YOU'LL NEVER BE ONE OF US. ALL YOU'LL EVER BE IS A TURTLE.
THAT'S WHY YOU HAVE THE WORST JUNK IN HERE, THE GOPHER. IT'S TRASH JUST LIKE YOU!
I HAD TO PROVE THOSE BRATS WRONG
WOW!! I'M IMPRESSED MASEGO, AFTER A YEAR'S WORK YOU FIXED THE GOPHER. IT EVEN OUTPERFORMED MY KID'S MECHA'S. JUST DON'T LOSE IT SO OFTEN
BUT THEN THEY DID THIS
WHY CAN'T YOU JUST STAY IN YOUR LANE. YOU CAN'T FIX GOPHER BETTER THAN OUR MECHA'S. GOPHER'S MANUAL IS TOO COMPLEX, 1000 PAGES LONG!
WE HACKED YOUR FILE. WE KNOW YOU HAVE DYSLEXIA, SO WE'LL FIX GOPHER FOR YOU AND DON'T DREAM OF RATTING ON US PUNK. WE'RE ENTABENI'S!
SYSTEM WARNING: T4N FUEL CELL OVERLOAD! CRISIS IMMINENT!!!
NOO! STOP IT!!

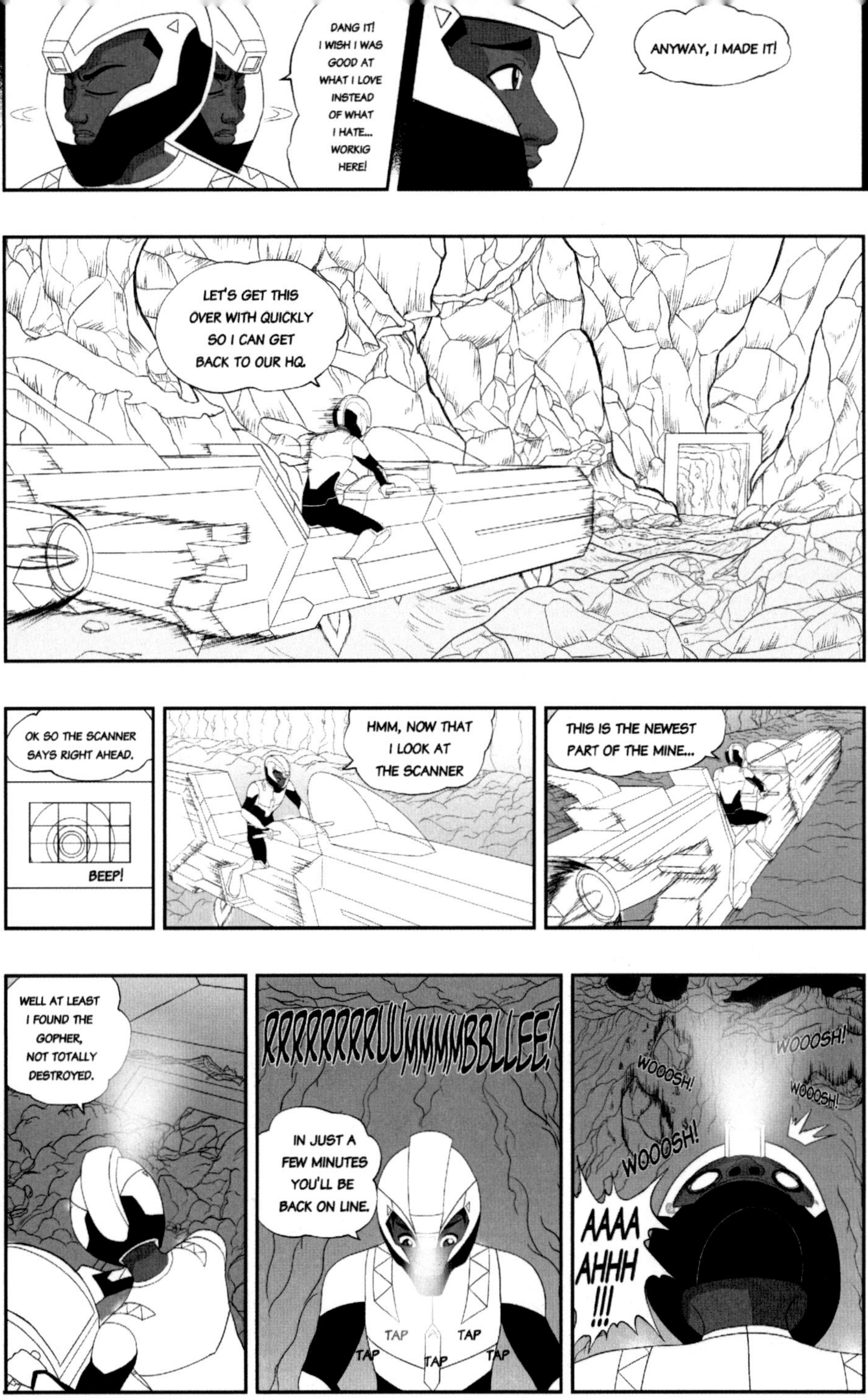
DANG IT! I WISH I WAS GOOD AT WHAT I LOVE INSTEAD OF WHAT I HATE... WORKIG HERE!
ANYWAY, I MADE IT!
LET'S GET THIS OVER WITH QUICKLY SO I CAN GET BACK TO OUR HQ.
OK SO THE SCANNER SAYS RIGHT AHEAD.
BEEP!
HMM, NOW THAT I LOOK AT THE SCANNER
THIS IS THE NEWEST PART OF THE MINE...
WELL AT LEAST I FOUND THE GOPHER, NOT TOTALLY DESTROYED.
RRRRRRRRRUUMMMMBBLLEE!
IN JUST A FEW MINUTES YOU'LL BE BACK ON LINE.
TAP TAP TAP TAP TAP
WOOOSH! WOOOSH! WOOOSH! WOOOSH!
AAAA AHHH !!!

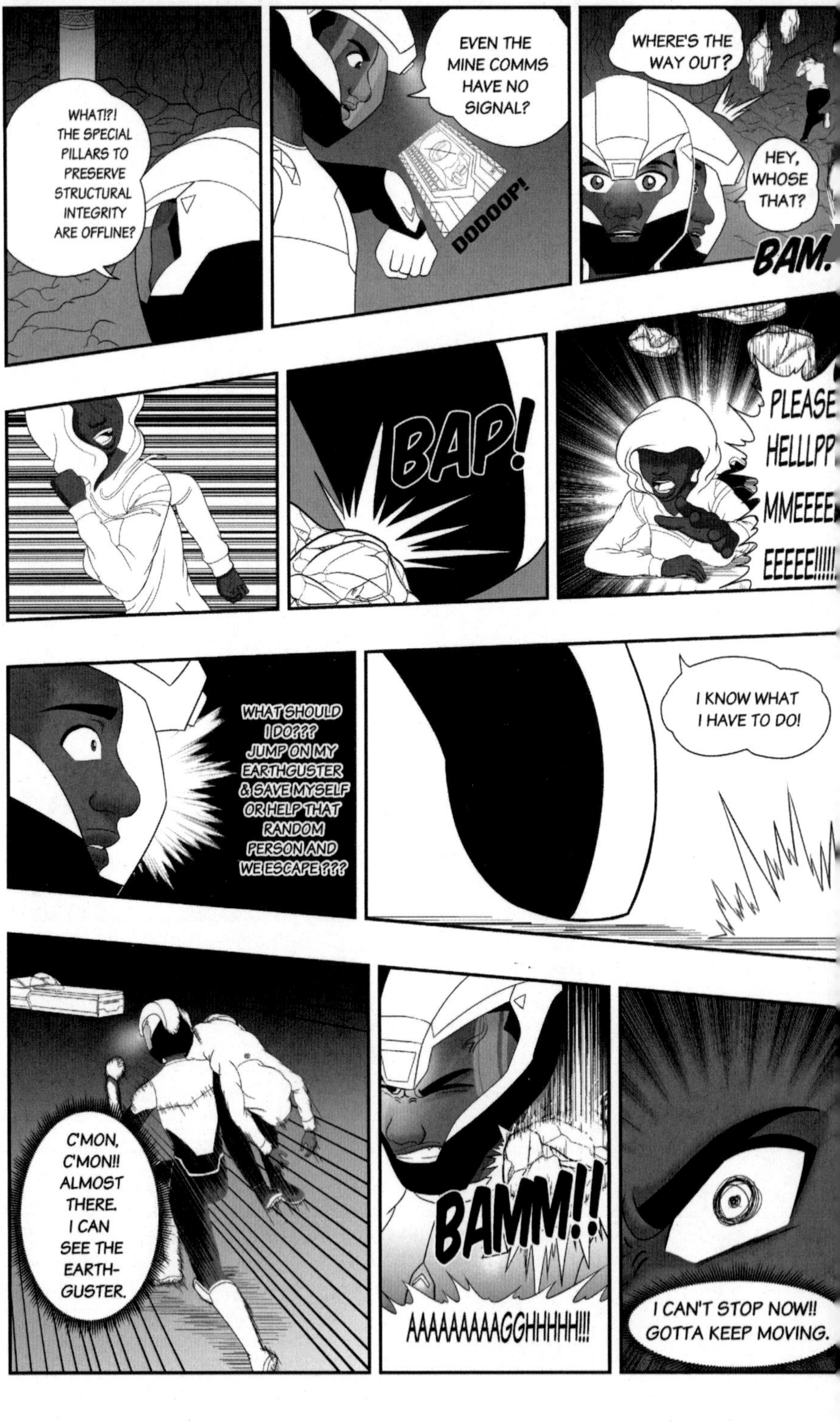
WHAT!?! THE SPECIAL PILLARS TO PRESERVE STRUCTURAL INTEGRITY ARE OFFLINE?
EVEN THE MINE COMMS HAVE NO SIGNAL?
DODOOP!
WHERE'S THE WAY OUT?
HEY, WHOSE THAT?
BAM.
BAP!
PLEASE HELLLPP MMEEEEEEEEE!!!!!
WHAT SHOULD I DO??? JUMP ON MY EARTHGUSTER & SAVE MYSELF OR HELP THAT RANDOM PERSON AND WE ESCAPE???
I KNOW WHAT I HAVE TO DO!
C'MON, C'MON!! ALMOST THERE. I CAN SEE THE EARTH-GUSTER.
BAMM!!
AAAAAAAAAGGHHHHH!!!
I CAN'T STOP NOW!! GOTTA KEEP MOVING.

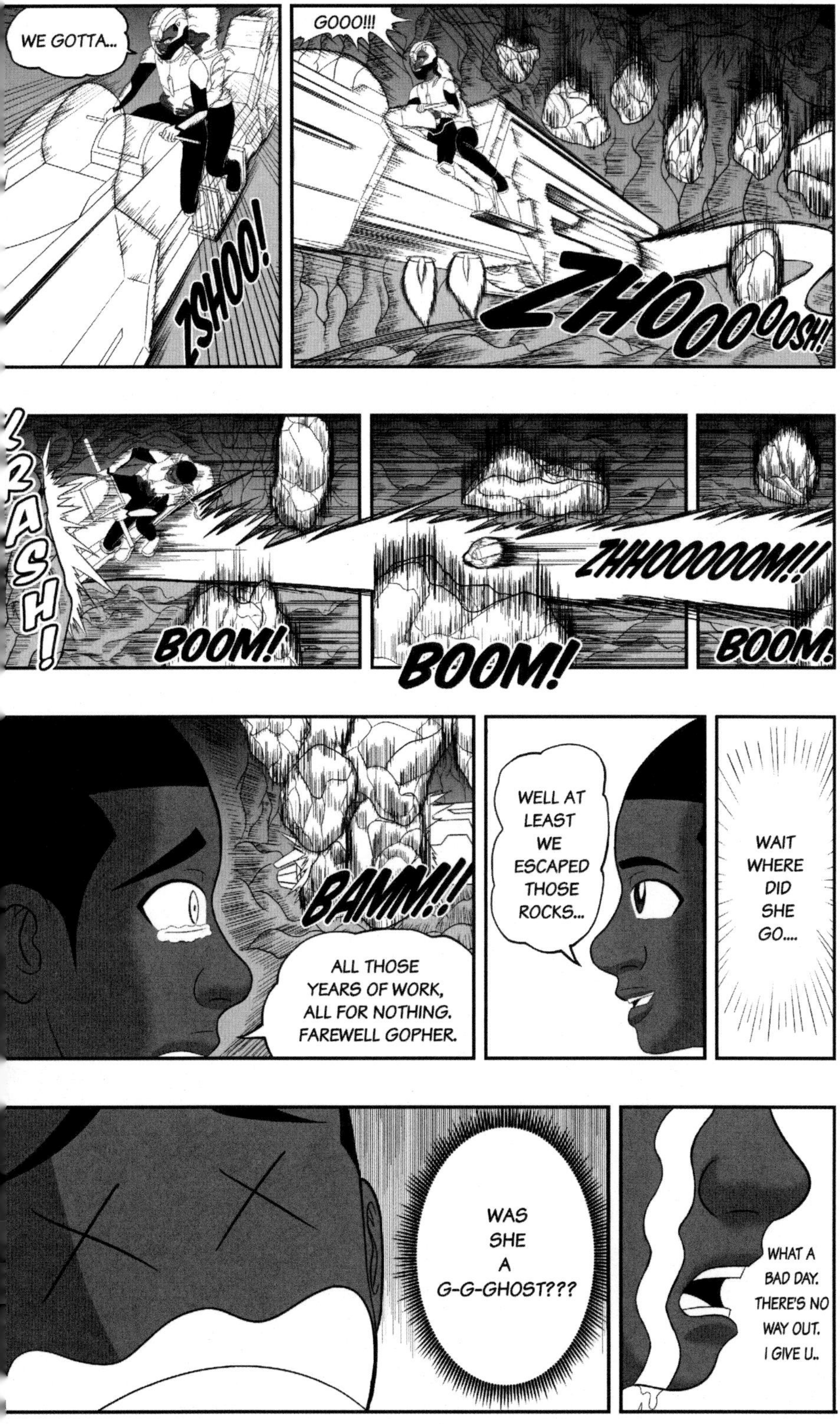
WE GOTTA...
ZSHOO!
GOOO!!!
ZHOOOOOOSH!
CRASH!
BOOM!
ZHHOOOOOOM!!
BOOM!
BOOM!
BAMM!!
ALL THOSE YEARS OF WORK, ALL FOR NOTHING. FAREWELL GOPHER.
WELL AT LEAST WE ESCAPED THOSE ROCKS...
WAIT WHERE DID SHE GO....
WAS SHE A G-G-GHOST???
WHAT A BAD DAY. THERE'S NO WAY OUT. I GIVE U..

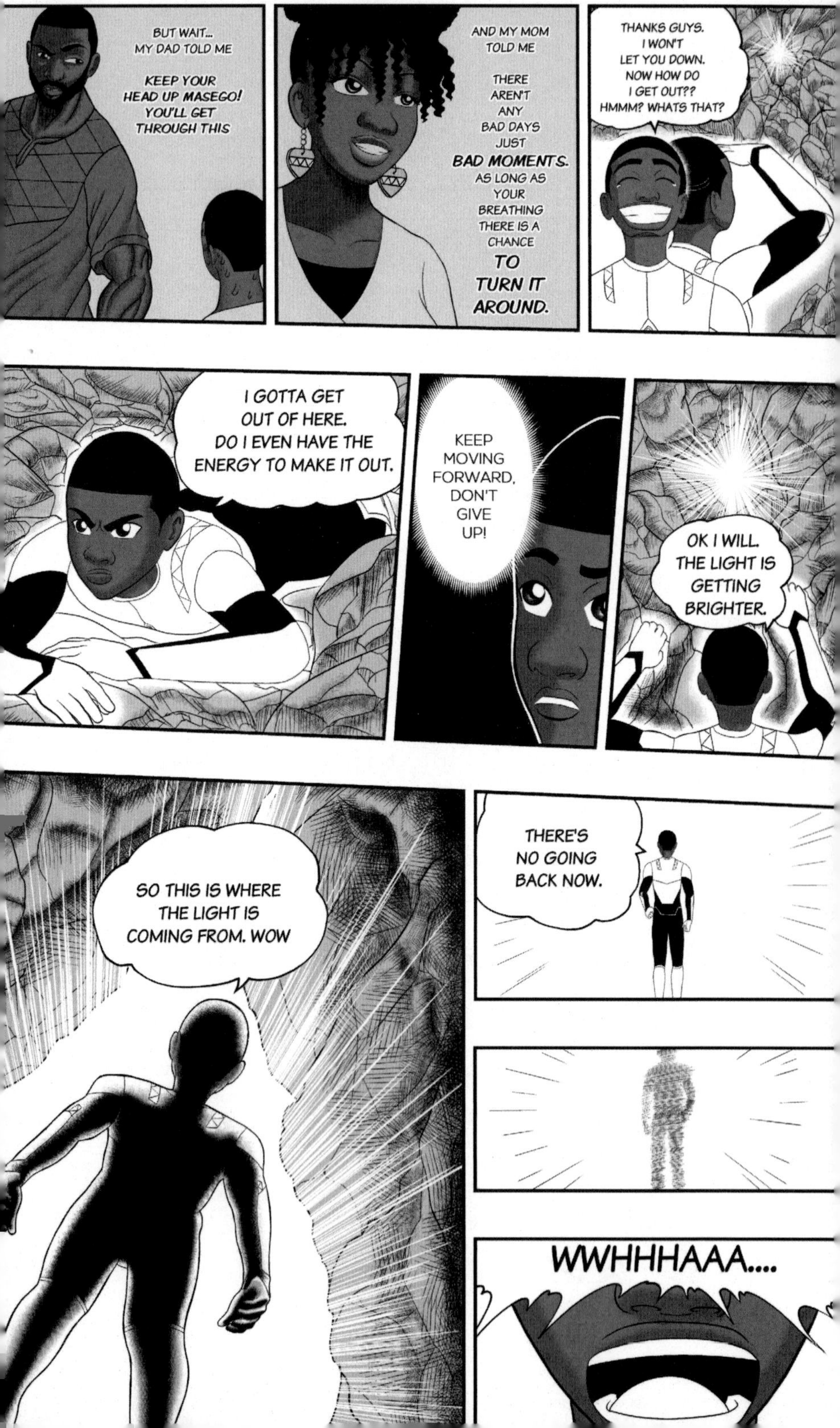
BUT WAIT... MY DAD TOLD ME
KEEP YOUR HEAD UP MASEGO! YOU'LL GET THROUGH THIS
AND MY MOM TOLD ME
THERE AREN'T ANY BAD DAYS JUST BAD MOMENTS. AS LONG AS YOUR BREATHING THERE IS A CHANCE TO TURN IT AROUND.
THANKS GUYS. I WON'T LET YOU DOWN. NOW HOW DO I GET OUT?? HMMM? WHATS THAT?
I GOTTA GET OUT OF HERE. DO I EVEN HAVE THE ENERGY TO MAKE IT OUT.
KEEP MOVING FORWARD, DON'T GIVE UP!
OK I WILL. THE LIGHT IS GETTING BRIGHTER.
SO THIS IS WHERE THE LIGHT IS COMING FROM. WOW
THERE'S NO GOING BACK NOW.
WWHHHAAA....

THIS IS AWESOME! SO MANY CRYSTALS! AND WHAT'S THAT?
WHAT'S THIS SAY?
...SEPARATES THE...
SEPARATES WHAT? MAYBE THIS THING CAN HELP?
HERE GOES EVERYTHING!
WELCOME BRAVE SOUL.YOU HAVE BEEN CHOSEN FOR THE DESTINY GATE BASED ON YOUR CHARACTER! THESE ANCIENT TESTS OCCUR EVERY FEW CENTURIES TO THOSE WHO SHOW GREAT PROMISE. IT'S PURPOSE IS TO SEPARATE THE STRONG FROM THE WEAK! THE TEST HAS ONLY ONE QUESTION! ANSWER IT CORRECTLY AND EARN GREAT POWER. FAIL AND LOSE WHAT MATTERS MOST! NOW HERE IS YOUR QUESTION.
I HAVE A GOOD FRIEND, WHO IS TEACHING ME A LOT OF THINGS, BUT UNFORTUNATELY MY FRIEND IS NOT SPEAKING. WHO IS MY FRIEND?
YOU HAVE 40 SECONDS!
I CAN'T BELIEVE IT. THAT MYTH THEY TOLD ME ABOUT YEARS AGO... WAS REAL!
HMM? WHO IS MY FRIEND? WHO?
24 SECONDS LEFT

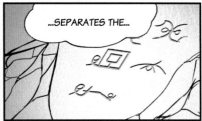

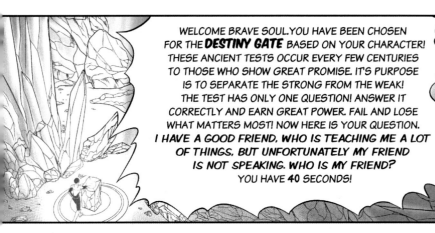

I'VE TAKEN TOO MANY L'S FOR THE DAY & I REFUSE TO TAKE ANOTHER.
10 SECONDS LEFT
I HAVE 2 ANSWERS
MY GUT SAYS...
A BOOK. NAH, THAT'S DUMB...
3 SECONDS LEF
MY MIND SAYS LIFE. WHICH IS IT???
AAGGGH I CAN'T TAKE THIS...
MY ANSWER IS A BOOK!!
1 SECOND LEFT
HA HA HA WELL DONE
MMMM...WHY DOES THAT HOOD LOOK FAMILIAR?
I AM CHINEDU, AN ANGEL & GUARDIAN MESSENGER OF BABA WA MWANGA! WHAT IS YOUR NAME?
I'M MASEGO UMNATHA! WHY DO I FEEL LIKE I'VE SEEN YOU BEFORE??
YOU HAVE, I'VE BEEN MONITORING YOU FOR SOME TIME MASEGO...
FROM YOUR FIRST RITE OF PASSAG TO WHEN YOU RISKED YOUR LIFE TO SAVE THAT WOMAN FROM THE CAVE-IN OUTSIDE!
THEN WAS THAT...?

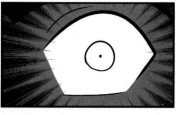

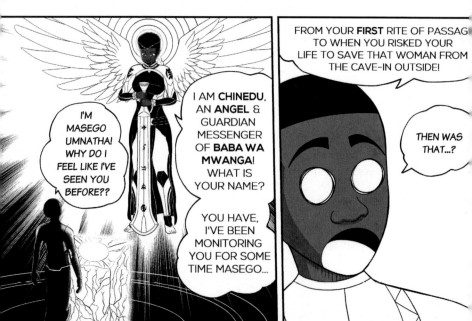

YES, I WAS THERE FROM THE START...

YEAR 1

...THIS WAS A **TEST** TO SEE YOUR CHOICE IN CRISIS...

I KNEW THAT WAS ODD!

...THAT'S WHY THE SIGN OUTSIDE SAYS **POWER SEPARATES THE STRONG FROM THE WEAK!**

THE WEAK CHOICE WOULD BE TO SAVE YOURSELF WHEN YOU HAVE THE POWER TO SAVE ANOTHER.

YOU SHOWED GREATNESS BY SERVING OTHERS.

WITH ALL THESE ATTRIBUTES YOU UNLOCKED THE DESTINY GATE!

YOUR PRIZE IS THE **UKUSA* FRUIT!**

ZHHIIING!

...THE DOOR TO ANCIENT POWER, RESERVED FOR THE WORTHY! IT UTILIZES THREADS, KNOWN AS **VIBRANT VERSATILE SILK** OR **VVS.**

FWHOOOSH!

*UKUSA IS THE XHOSA TERM FOR "DAWN"

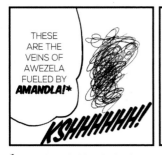

THESE ARE THE VEINS OF AWEZELA FUELED BY **AMANDLA!***

KSHHHHHH!

MOST ONLY GAIN THE UKUSA SEED. BUT YOU GAINED FRUIT & SEED!

MASEGO, EXIT THE ORDINARY AND ENTER THE EXTRAORDINARY!

*AMANDLA IS THE XHOSA TERM FOR "POWER"

CRUNCH

TZZSSH

HHHOOO!!

NOW THE NEXT STEP IS TO FOCUS YOUR MIND... ENVISION A PROTECTIVE LAYER OVER YOUR ENTIRE BODY!

KSHHHUUU

I DID IT! HOW DOES THIS WORK?

ALWAYS REMEMBER WHAT YOU THINK & SPEAK BECOME REALITY.

THAT IS THE KEY TO THE UKUSA FRUIT AND THE RELIC. REMEMBER THIS & THRIVE!

BNNN

DOOM!!

BWHOOOM!!

WAIT, I HAVE SO MANY MORE QUESTIONS...

WHERE ARE YOU SENDING ME!?! WHAT IF I NEED YOUR HELP!?!

FEAR NOT! WE SHALL MEET AGAIN! BRAVE ONWARDS LIMIT DESTROYER!

VSSHHH

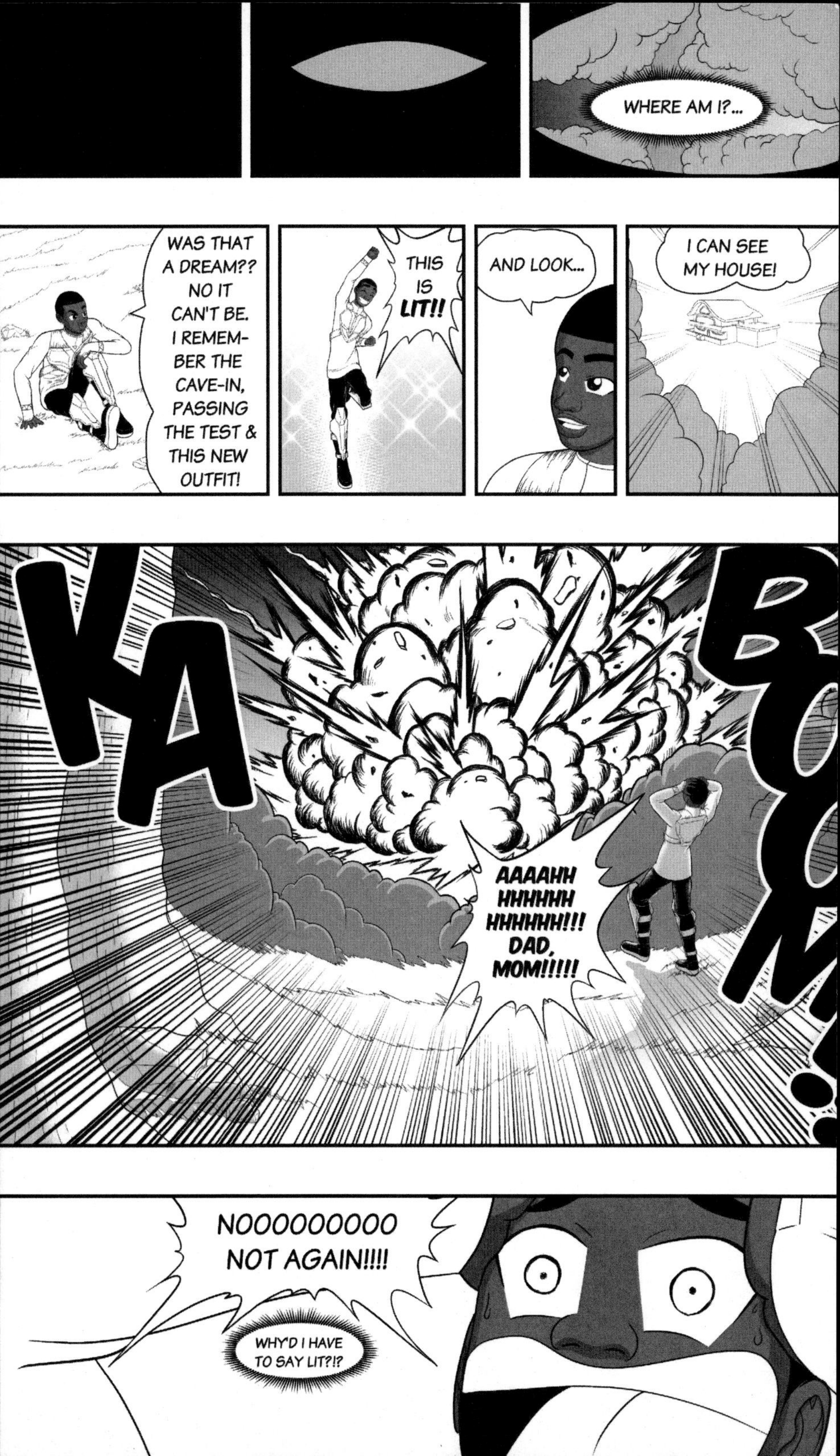
WHERE AM I?...
WAS THAT A DREAM?? NO IT CAN'T BE. I REMEMBER THE CAVE-IN, PASSING THE TEST & THIS NEW OUTFIT!
THIS IS LIT!!
AND LOOK...
I CAN SEE MY HOUSE!
KA
BOOM!!
AAAAHH HHHHHH HHHHHH!!! DAD, MOM!!!!!
NOOOOOOOOO NOT AGAIN!!!!
WHY'D I HAVE TO SAY LIT?!?

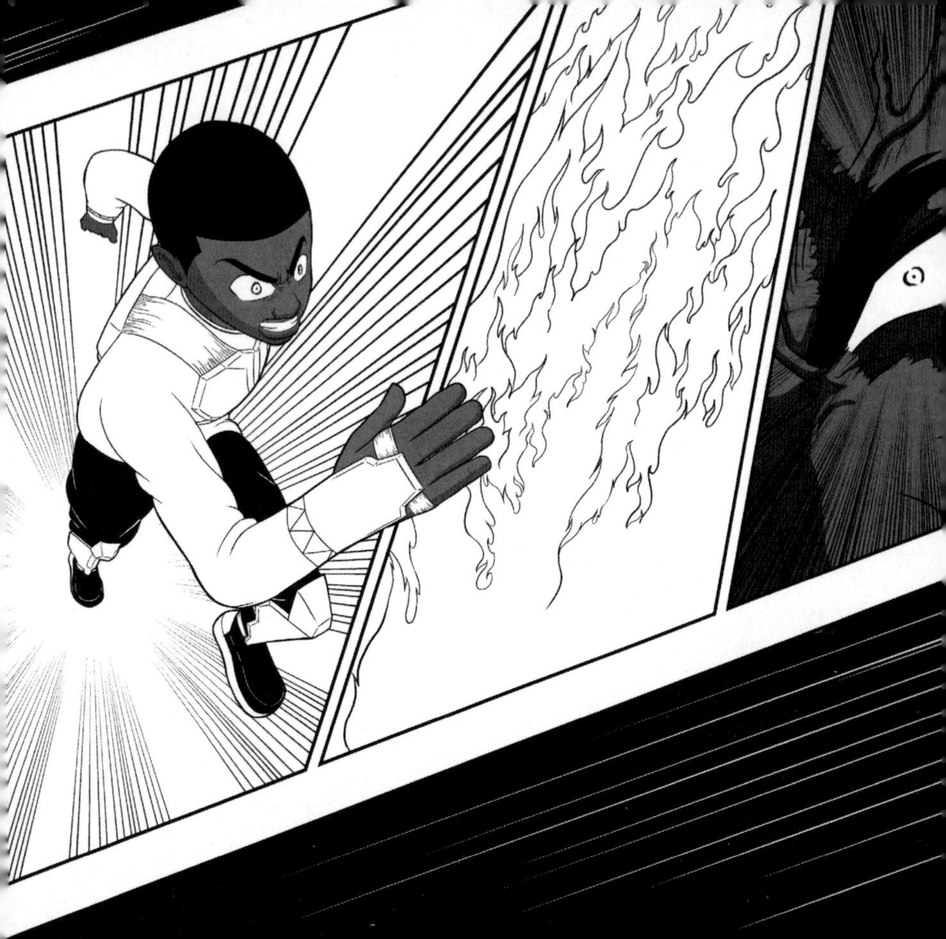

MASEGO'S RACE AGAINST TIME

AFTER FINALLY CONQUERING THE DESTINY GATE MASEGO IS ON CLOUD 9!
HOWEVER LIFE FLINGS HIM BACK TO EARTH WHEN HIS PARENTS HOUSE IS ATTACKED.
CAN HE MAKE IT BACK IN TIME TO RESCUE THEM? WHO STARTED THIS ASSAULT?
WILL HIS NEWFOUND POWER HELP OR HINDER HIM?

FIND OUT IN THE NEXT EXPLOSIVE CHAPTER OF

BOLD SAGA

BRAVE ONWARDS LIMIT DESTROYER

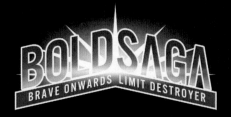

MASEGO UMNATHA

A TIMID 15 YEAR OLD TEEN UNASHAMED TO GO ALL OUT TO FULFILL HIS DREAM & HONOR A PROMISE, MASEGO HAS PASSION. ALTHOUGH HE ENJOYS TECH, MUSIC AND ART HIS #1 GOAL IS TO BECOME THE NEXT WARRIOR KING, THE ANANSI. INSPITE OF THE VICISSITUDES OF LIFE TRYING TO DESTROY HIS HOPE, HE PERSISTED. THUS, HE PREVAILED AND BRAVELY WALKS THROUGH THE DESTINY GATE, EMBARKING ON A NEW SAGA...

RITE OF PASSAGE

TO JOIN NEBULA ONE OF THE REQUIREMENTS IS A RITE OF PASSAGE . IT INVOLVES 1 WRITTEN TEST AND **2** ROUNDS OF PHYSICAL COMBAT. ROUND 1 IS NGUNI STICK FIGHTING. IT CONSISTS OF AN ISIKHWILI OR ATTACKING STICK, AN UBHOKU OR DEFENDING STICK AND IHAWU, OR DEFENDING SHIELD. TO WIN A MATCH ONE FIGHTER MUST LAND A DECISIVE BLOW ON THEIR OPPONENT WITHOUT BEING BLOCKED BY THEIR SHIELD. ALTHOUGH THIS MARTIAL ART OCCURS IN THIS STORY'S RITE OF PASSAGE SOME BELIEVE IT ORIGINATED AND WAS PRACTICED BY SHAKA ZULU DURING HIS REIGN. FORMER SOUTH AFRICAN PRESIDENT, NELSON MANDELA WAS A PRACTITIONER OF THIS MARTIAL ART. ROUND **2** IS MUSANGWE, A BARE KNUCKLE BOXING MARTIAL ART THAT ORIGINATED FROM THE VENDA PEOPLE OF AFRICA. TO WIN A FIGHTER MUST: MAKE THEIR OPPONENT BLEED, GET THEM KNOCKED OUT OR SURRENDER.

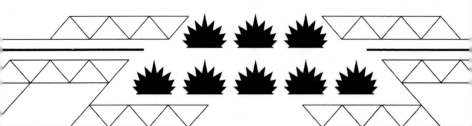

AWEZELA EMPIRE

UKUZOLA VILLAGE

THE KINGDOM OF AWEZELA IS AN INCREDIBLE TERRITORY THAT IS OVERFLOWING WITH ADVANCED TECHNOLOGY, GREAT CULTURE AND GENERALLY PEACEFUL. IT WAS FORMED CENTURIES AGO AFTER THE SHAKA ZULU AND HIS IMPI WARRIORS DEFEATED THE DREADED ISITHUNZI EMPIRE AND SEALED THEM AWAY... AT THE HEART OF THE INNOVATION IS THE THREAD OF THE KINGDOM, THE VIBRANT VERSATILE SILK OR VVS. IT POWERS TRANSPORATION, CREATES CLOTHING AND IS INTERWOVEN INTO EVERY ASPECT OF AWEZELAN LIFE. THE POWER OF THE VVS IS SO INFLUENTIAL IT HELPED AWEZELA GO FROM A SMALL KINGDOM ON EARTH TO A MAJESTIC EMPIRE SPANNING THE STARS. ALTHOUGH AWEZELA IS FICTIONAL IT IS INSPIRED BY THE REAL WORLD MUTAPA EMPIRE. THIS SOUTHERN AFRICAN KINGDOM CONTAINED PRESENT DAY ZIMBABWE, MOZAMBIQUE, SOUTH EASTERN NAMIBIA AND SOUTH AFRICA.IT WAS KNOWN FOR GOLD TRADE, TRADING PORTS AND STRUCTURE! THE EMPIRE WAS RULED ON MULTIPLE LEVELS, FROM THE VILLAGE ALL THE WAY UP TO THE CAPITAL. THE KINGDOM OF MUTAPA IS NOT COMMONLY USED IN STORIES, SO I DECIDED TO USE IT AS INSPIRATION TO FUEL MY STORY. SHOWCASING A CULTURE OF AFRICAN ROYALTY, PRESTIGE AND EXCELLENCE!

NEBULA

SINCE THOSE WHO ENLIST WITH
STAAR START TRAINING AT 15 A
NEW INSTITUTION WAS FORGED TO
ENLIST BRIGHT, RESILIENT MINDS.
IT BECAME KNOWN AS THE NEBULA,
ASTANDARD INSTITUTION THAT IS
THE PREREQUISITE FOR STAAR. IT'S
PURPOSE IS TO BIRTH GREATER
WARRIORS FOR THE NEXT
GENERATION. WITH INTENSE CURRI-
CULUM AND RIGID TRAINING YOUNG
STUDENTS ARE TRANSFORMED!
THEY BECOME SPECIALISTS WHO
FLOAT LIKE CLOUDS ABOVE ANY OB
STACLE. YET SHINE LIKE A NEBULA
IN A DARK AND CRUEL WORLD.
A GREAT STARTING PLACE
FOR STARS TO FORM.

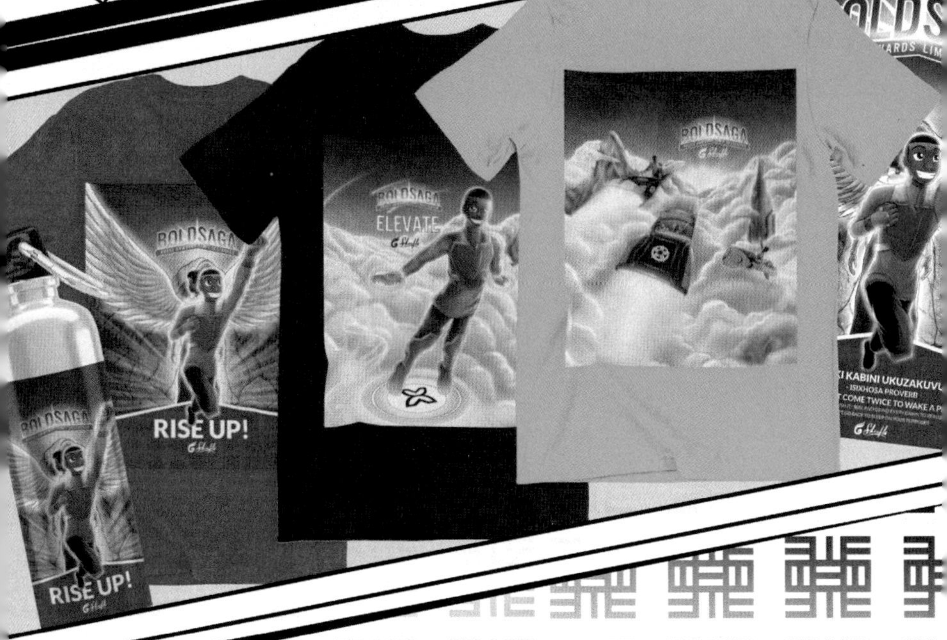
BOLDSAGA
RISE UP!
BOLDSAGA
ELEVATE
BOLDSAGA
RISE UP!

DARE TO BE BOLD

IN A WORLD OF ORDINARY DARE TO BE EXTRAORDINARY! ENTER BOLDSAGA, AN AFROFUTURISTIC MANGA THAT FOLLOWS MASEGO AND FRIENDS ON THE SEARCH FOR AN ANCIENT RELIC TO VANQUISH AN EVIL EMPIRE SPREAD ACROSS THE GALAXIES!

IN ADDITION SHOP AMAZING STYLES THAT LOOK GREAT AND INSPIRE GREATNESS.
CLICK THE LINK **WWW.GREATGALE.COM/BOLDSAGA** TO FIND MAJESTIC HAND DRAWN ILLUSTRATIONS, EXCLUSIVELY FRESH T-SHIRTS, APPAREL, ACCESSORIES & MORE FOR YOU! SUPPORT THIS BLACK OWNED BUSINESS CREATING CHANGE!

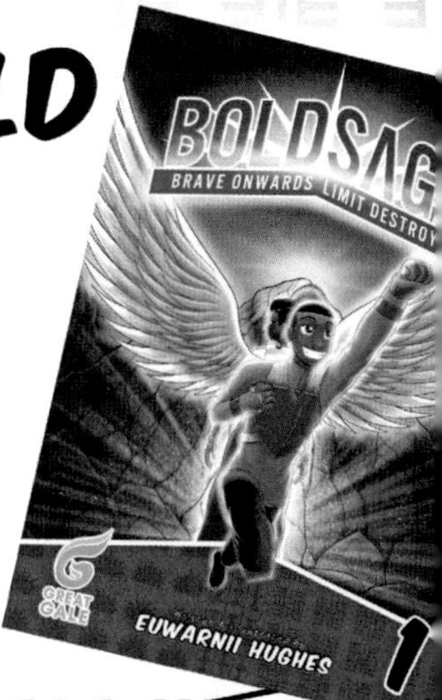
BOLDSAGA
BRAVE ONWARDS LIMIT DESTROY
GREAT GALE
EUWARNII HUGHES
1

SHOP TODAY

WWW.GREATGALE.COM/BOLDSAGA

FOLLOW US FOR MORE: @GREATGALECO
@GREATGALESHEAFLO

CONTACT US AT: MAIL.BOLDSAGA@GMAIL.COM

Made in the USA
Las Vegas, NV
16 July 2021